SASQUATCH RACE

HIDDEN MOUNTAIN CHRONICLES
BOOK 1

PATRICK TALMADGE

HANGAR 1 PUBLISHING

This book is dedicated to Coni for motivating and helping me reach my goal.

1

What *does Coach want this time?*

Jack walked slowly toward the state-of-the-art gym on campus where he'd be meeting his track coach. He passed the red brick college buildings dating back to 1895 and walked through the central square with students sprawled on the lawn in the spring sun.

Clenching his fist he thought, *Why can't she stop interfering with my life and drop the touchy-feely stuff? I haven't lost a race in two years, so why does she keep nosing into my life? Can't she see I just want to be left alone?*

It had been two years since the car accident and Coach Sulli kept trying to get him to deal with his feelings over what happened. Jack always countered with a cocky, "I'm doing alright, aren't I?" as she looked at him with concern in her steely gray eyes.

A junior, he had the highest ranking of any runner in the country. With only one year left before he'd get his degree, he just wanted to get it over with without dealing with the feelings that he kept locked up tight.

She probably won't drop it, no matter what I say.

As he opened the doors of the new gym, he thought about how he was going to miss this gleaming facility. Not long after the accident, an anonymous alumni donated funds to build the gym, the track, and even more money for athletic scholarships. People said the college was lucky, but Jack had always thought somehow it was meant to keep him in school after the accident.

Coach Sulli's office door was at the end of the hall of trophies. She had won dozens by herself and while on a relay team. One of the best middle-distance runners in the world in her day, no woman in the history of the college had matched any of Sulli's times. At forty-six, Sulli was the fastest woman in the world in master's track and field running in the 800m and 1500m. Heck, Sulli could still outrun every girl on the team.

Sulli's door was always open, that is unless someone was getting a butt chewing. And Jack had his share of those closed-door motivational meetings over the years with Sulli.

He stepped into the doorway, paused, and said, "Hi Coach."

"Hi Jack," Sulli responded without looking up from her paperwork. "Close the door and take a seat, will you?" She looked up, "You know why I called you here today, don't you?" Then she added, "And, by the way, Happy Birthday!"

Somehow Sulli managed to keep track of the details of her runners' lives. He hesitated, and then quietly said, "Thanks. An uh, you want me to feel my feelings and contact my relatives, right?"

A smile wrinkled the corner of her eyes. "That's right, but this year I'm asking even more."

"What more could you be asking for?"

Sulli caught and held Jack's eye for the first time since he entered her office. Her tone belonged to a typical, no-nonsense coach, but her eyes betrayed a softness and deep empathy toward Jack. Sometimes, Jack felt Sulli was the mom he needed for support and understanding. She had always helped him through his low times, and today she was probably going to try to make him feel better.

"Jack," Sulli began with a brisk tone to her voice. "You have run another great season, but your heart is not in it. You only run to win. You never push yourself except in practice."

She must have seen his face close up because Sulli added, "Do not give me that look. I know you have not lost a race since the accident, but you have not had your mind on any race since then either. All you do is go to school and run. Jack, you are running three workouts a day, seven days a week, with no breaks, and you have been doing that since the accident. Yes, I know you have won every race, but you do not race, you just win."

Jack opened his mouth to answer her, but Sulli held her hand up to stop him before he got a word out. "Jack, you are the best runner the country has ever seen, but you run without a soul. You do not show your feelings at all when you run. The team is worried about you, and it affects them more than you know. Your attitude brings people around you down, even when you win.

"I remember your passion for running when you were in high school and your first year here before the accident. You used to be excited every time you ran, regardless of whether it was a race or a workout. That Jack is not showing up anymore."

Jack just looked at her through lifeless eyes. He knew very well what she was talking about.

"I have spoken to Doc Mayo about this, and we have decided on a plan of action for you. You need a break from school and running."

Jack stood up, gripping the back of his chair briefly before beginning to pace back and forth.

Coach Sulli watched him, then said, "As you know, your lawyer has been trying to contact you for weeks. Finally, he called me to make sure you did not miss the important meeting today. As soon as you leave my office, you are going to Doc Mayo's office for a talk, and then she is driving you to your family house to meet with your lawyer. We will not take no for an answer this time, and you *will* follow our directions for the summer. To make sure you go home, I am forbidding you from being on school property for the summer. You cannot train here at school and will stay off campus until the fall semester starts," Sulli said.

"Yes, cross country begins in three months, so you'd better produce a suitable alternative. I expect you to follow everything Doc Mayo and I have planned. Failure to follow our orders, and yes, they are orders, will result in your suspension from cross-country and track next season."

He finally erupted like a tightly coiled spring. "That's not right!" Jack shouted in a voice that could be heard down the hall. "What's the big deal? Why should I have to jump through hoops just to feel sad? How I feel is my business."

Sulli quickly answered, her pitch lowered to try to calm him. "I know this sounds rough, but it is for your good and the good of the team. Do not ask again, because no, you do not have a choice in the matter. Before you try to argue with me, take off for Doc Mayo's office, and I mean now!"

"But Coach . . ."

"No buts, Jack. I really care about you, but I'm tired of watching you live a hollow life. You are not helping the team even though you win every race you enter because everyone sees how hurt you are. Your lack of emotion affects them, their ability to train, and how well they compete. We want you to come back, but as a whole person, not just a fast runner. I want the excited kid I first met three years ago back. If you cannot do it for yourself, then do it for the team."

Jack couldn't think of one thing to say that would change anything. Reluctantly, he said, "OK, I will talk to Doc Mayo, but I am not happy." Then he remembered the meeting with the lawyer, and worried there might be a legal issue, tentatively, he asked, "Do you know what the lawyer wants?"

"Do not have a clue," Sulli said, "but he really was adamant about seeing you today. I would guess now that you are twenty-one it has something to do with your parents' estate, but I don't know for sure."

As Jack was turning to leave, Coach Sulli called his name. Jack turned and saw as Coach Sulli pulled something out of her desk, stood up, and handed Jack a small box with a smile, "Open it."

Inside, Jack found a cool, expensive-looking watch with a techno look. Jack stared at it, he'd never seen anything like it before.

Sulli laughed and said, "Try it on for size."

As Jack was putting the watch on, Sulli explained about the company that had asked her to give it to him. They wanted him to evaluate it privately and off-season before it was introduced to the public. They had passed on the instruction that he shouldn't even talk to anyone about the watch. In return for him testing it, the company would pledge to give every athlete in the college one. Sulli finished, asking Jack, "Do you want to try it out?"

"Heck yes, I will! My watch is old, and this one looks like it can do about everything but cook."

Sulli laughed and said there was a booklet that explained how it worked, but the company rep explained it worked like normal watches, so it would be easy to use. It had everything every other top-running GPS watches had, except its battery lasted for years without charging. The watch was wafer thin and so light Jack could hardly feel it on his wrist. The watch face was large, and the display data was easy to read, but the weightlessness made him curious.

"Thanks, Coach," Jack said as he checked the watch, and walked out of her office with a smile on his face.

2

As Jack made his way to Doc Mayo's office, he thought about all the time he had spent with her. He hated talking to Doc Mayo. She was able to look right through him, and he always found it hard to think around her. She started at the college right after the accident to help him adjust and never left. There was something familiar about her that he couldn't put his finger on. It wasn't that it was unpleasant talking to her, but she was another one who always wanted him to connect with his feelings.

As he walked, glancing down at his shiny timepiece again, Jack tried to figure out why it was he could not seem to identify any of his feelings about the accident. Doc Mayo was easy to talk to, and Jack knew that, unlike him, his teammates really connected with her. She was one of the best sports psychologists, but he just couldn't seem to open up to her about the accident.

If it were not for the Doc, my life would be simpler, Jack thought. At his appointments every few weeks, Doc Mayo tried to get him to open up about his feelings. The only feelings he had were why her black eyes and long dark hair made him stare.

Suddenly, Jack stopped walking and smiled. Maybe Doc Mayo reminded him of Michelle! That's why he couldn't talk to her. Though he missed Michelle in the worst way, for reasons he didn't understand, he could not seem to muster up the courage to see her or even call her. Doc Mayo wouldn't understand, but he had worked his whole life to control his competitive feelings, and now the doc wanted him to be a sissy, bleeding heart with feelings coming out his ears.

Crap, what am I in for now? Jack wondered as he reached her building. As always Jack let himself into Doc Mayo's office. Today he said, "Hi Doc. Did you want to see me?"

"You know well enough I do, young man," she said. She always called him "young man", and she couldn't be more than ten years older than him. Damn, her intense black eyes immediately drew him right in and made him feel like she was definitely in control.

As Jack looked at the Doc, he thought, *Yes, her eyes remind me of Michelle's*. He'd never really thought about it until now, but Michelle looked Native American, except her eyes were green, instead of black like Doc's. Jack had grown up in the Native American culture, where black eyes were predominant, green rarer.

How could he have known Michelle for years and just now realized she looked Native American? Jack thought Michelle was the most beautiful woman he had ever seen.

Maybe she really is Native. Maybe that was why his Uncle Mick had kept her around so long, smiling at the thought. Mick was always helping other tribal members. He really needed to go see Michelle after finishing with the lawyer. No way Michelle is Native American, or Uncle Mick would have bragged about it. He was always bragging about how Natives were the best humans in the world.

I can't believe I haven't called her once, let alone visited her for two years. Michelle is going to kick my butt when she sees me . . . if she is still there. What reason could she have for staying on after Mick's death? *Oh my God, what if she's left, and I can't find her?*

Doc Mayo interrupted Jack's thoughts of Michelle by saying, "Jack it looks like this is the end of your avoidance road. I have tried talking to you nicely for the last two years, and you would not open up to me at all."

"So, what makes you think anything has changed now?"

"OK, Lobo, enough banter. Sit down and let's go over the plan."

As Doc Mayo's eyes seemed to bore right into his soul as Jack thought, *Wait, did she just call me Lobo?* Why was she using that name? She had never done that before . . . Worse yet, she sounded just like his uncle Mick when he was trying to get Jack to listen.

"Jack, I know Coach Sulli told you a little bit about what we are expecting of you, but not everything. As we both know, two years ago today you experienced a terrible personal blow with the accident that took the lives of your family. You have avoided dealing with any part of the accident. You've hidden out from the world, and your remaining family and friends.

"Sulli and I have talked. We've decided it is time to push you in the right direction. First, you need to get away from school. It's time you went back to your house even if just for this meeting. You also need to step back into your old life for a while, to take care of this unfinished family business with your lawyer."

Jack hung his head, avoiding her direct look. "This really sucks, Doc."

"Jack, please understand, we are not trying to hurt you by making you face up to your responsibilities. If you do not do these things for yourself, you will never heal, and you will continue to hide from life. As a result, you will not be able to reach your full potential, and you will not run the way you want to. What we are asking of you is going to make your life better. We have some ideas of what we think you should do while you are away from school, but you can decide for yourself after we speak with the lawyer.

"First, go over the outline of what I think you should do over the next three months, and then we are going to your family house to meet with your lawyer. You have not set foot in that house since the accident. It's time for you to meet those demons head-on."

Doc Mayo looked at Jack who still had his head lowered, and continued, her voice steady and kind. "That's why I am going with you to the house, Jack. I know you are serious, as always, about your summer classes. As you will soon see, I pulled strings to allow you to take a special class off campus. Consider this class your reward."

At the word "reward" Jack lifted his head to see Doc Mayo was looking at him with a smile.

"You are registered for an individual contract class that will allow you to do all your work away from campus and turn the paperwork in at the end of the summer. It is a pass-fail class, so no worry about your straight A's even if you lay out in the sun for the summer doing nothing—although I doubt that will happen," Doc Mayo said.

"Right now, I want you to go to your dorm room and gather everything you will need for the next three months. Coach Sulli and I are not kidding when we say you are not to return until the first day of fall classes. We told the other athletes you will be gone for the summer and will not return until the first day of school. That also means no early-season cross-country practices. They know you and trust you will be there for practice the first day of school—no sooner —so don't worry about them.

"By the way, I heard some are saying they might have a chance to beat you if you take the summer off. See, Lobo, your being away for the summer is already showing healthier behavior from your teammates."

There goes my nickname again. Why does she keep calling me Lobo?

Doc Mayo continued, seemingly pleased with the situation. "I assume you will want to bring all your running gear and personal items. As for the rest of what you should bring, you must figure that out for yourself." Doc Mayo handed Jack a packet, "Here is the summer class we picked for you. I am sure you will love it."

"Only one class?" he asked, his eyebrows raised.

She smiled, "You heard right. One class, but it has the credits of a full load."

Jack looked down at the front cover sheet that read "Advanced Gene Theories of Humanoids and Diverse Animals of the Pacific Northwest." *All right*, he thought. At least his summer class work was going to be interesting.

"OK, Lobo, head out of here and go gather your things. I'll pick you up in front of your dorm in an hour. Do not even think of hiding because I will find your sorry butt."

As Jack walked away the name Lobo reverberated in his head. Why now, of all times, would Doc Mayo start calling him Lobo? She knew of his nickname—it was in his files—but had never used it before. Weird, but who could figure Doc Mayo out?

As he headed back toward the dorm, he was thinking about the summer class they picked.

How had they convinced Dr. Ellis to agree to that class? Jack had tried to get permission to do an independent study on that subject for the past two years. Doc Ellis always said that area of study was not based on true science. A scientist needed grounding in the real world.

Jack, growing up in the Native American culture, knew his studies during and after college were not going to follow normal Western scientific thoughts or directions. He wanted to study nature and how it managed to survive so well without humans helping.

In his dorm room, Jack quickly sorted his clothes and gear and shoved them into totes. He stopped and looked around his stripped dorm room, thinking about the last two years and about this second disappointing track season. Sure, he had won every cross-country and track race, but Coach Sulli was right, he was running without heart. He knew it was time to quit screwing around. He needed to spend the summer training and try to find his reason for running again.

As he hauled a tote and his gear to the elevator, Jack knew something was missing in his life. He really did not want to live through another emotionless season like he had just gone through. Coach Sulli was right and so was Doc Mayo. Though they had not said much with their words during the season, their eyes spoke volumes. He knew they cared.

Jack knew he'd have to spend the summer working out harder than he had ever worked to reignite his passion for running again. The goal was to return to school in the fall with his head screwed on right, have the best cross-country season the college had ever seen, and follow that up with a fantastic track season. He had to make it up to the coaches and the team.

The goal he kept in front of him was to make the Olympic team after he graduated. Jack knew if he continued to run the way he had run the last two years he would make the Olympic team, but he did not know if he would enjoy running in them the way he felt now.

Something needs to change in my life—big time—so I can fall in love with running again.

3

Jack was a small-town boy in a big city college. His first year of college was a revelation. He learned about the real world in college but preferred his simpler small-town life.

With only fifty students in his kindergarten through high school combined, coming to college was a shock to his system. Although he earned top grades, he found distractions everywhere.

Growing up, he had been sheltered as his parents had been strict and strait-laced. They didn't drink and didn't allow him to date until his senior year in high school. With so few girls in his class, there wasn't much choice, and he didn't date a lot.

He first met Michelle at Uncle Mick's house and immediately had a crush on her. He wondered if it was what they call "love at first sight," because from the moment he first laid eyes on her, he knew she was the one for him. She was the most incredible girl he had ever met, and he just hoped she would like a geek like him.

During his first year at college, he encountered pot—which he had never seen before, let alone smelled back home. All you had to do was knock on a door in the frat house to score pot to smoke. Jack tried it once but decided, even though it was fun, it was not for him.

He needed his lungs for running, and he wanted to do more than just sit on his butt playing video games.

Beer and most anything else you wanted to drink was even easier to access. The three refrigerators in the kitchen were full of beer, wine, and mixers for the hard stuff in the bar. But Jack did not want to take a chance on screwing up his life by drinking. Mom, Dad, and Uncle Mick made sure he knew the risks. Mick really drummed into his head how it would mess up his running.

Jack didn't know what to think when Mick also used to tell him, "Your crazy, rare blond hair and blue eyes are a sign that you are destined to be the next great shaman after me." Mick also used to tease him, saying, "No shaman in the history of our nation has ever drunk alcohol, and I'm not going to have you be the first."

Too bad I'm not Native American, or I could really be a shaman, Jack often thought. He wished he hadn't been adopted. At an early age, his parents told him about his adoption. Life would have been so much simpler if he just had been Native American like Mom and Dad and his Uncle Mick.

As Jack hauled another tote downstairs and a duffel bag, he thought about what he'd do next. Maybe the best way to train would be to go up into the mountains away from TV, the internet, girls, parties, and all the other college-life distractions.

Maybe I'll go to Uncle Mick's cabin. It had been two years since he had last left campus or visited Mick's cabin on Mt. Rainier. He had never been to the cabin without Mick being there. Uncle Mick trained him up at that cabin every summer since Jack was a little kid. In fact, he had been going to the cabin since before he could walk. Every vacation and more weekends than he could count, he ran the trails up there.

He smiled when he thought of Uncle Mick and how he always told him he had what it takes to be the world's greatest runner.

He knew the cabin was the place to get his head back on straight. A summer away from the noisy frat parties and other distractions was just what the doctor ordered. Plus, there was a chance Michelle had decided to stay in the area. He thought about how great it would be to see her again.

Because the cabin was miles away from an affordable grocery store, Jack would have to take his basic food stuffs needed for the whole summer. The perishables he would buy in town once a week. The drive into the small town where Mick's café was located was about four miles, but he probably wouldn't drive the dirt road more than once a week. *That is, unless Michelle is still in town,* Jack thought as a smile came to his face. He would save his trips into town for fresh vegetables and a delicious meal if she was still at the café.

He planned to catch fish, do a little hunting, gather wild berries, maybe plant a little garden to supplement his diet, and keep busy between workouts. Jack remembered there was an old, abandoned farm a couple of miles down the road with fruit trees. He wanted to make sure he ate right to get the best out of the tough training he was about to put himself through. It took the whole hour Doc Mayo had given him to get all his school and training gear together and downstairs in front of the dorm. The last thing he grabbed was his small backpack stocked with emergency equipment. Uncle Mick taught him to always wear it when he was out of sight of the cabin. His dad used to tell him that high in the mountains the weather could change in just minutes, and if he got hurt, he needed to be able to take care of himself.

Jack had always argued, "I won't be able to run fast with it on," but his dad and Mick always said, "Either run with it on or don't go."

Long ago, he had designed a safe, but light, emergency pack. Then, three years earlier, he picked up a lightweight pack made from Kevlar, so it was super-strong, light, and bulletproof. Jack thought it would be strong enough to hold his weight if needed and loaded it as lightly as possible. He always used white sports tape for blisters and sprains, plus it worked great to seal cuts. The roll was big and bulky, so he rolled about twenty feet of it onto a toothpick—enough for emergencies without the added size.

In case he was stuck outside for the night, he needed to keep warm and dry, so he had brought a light waterproof jacket and pants, and long, silk underwear to wear underneath. The pants and top together were exceptionally light in a small package and would keep him warm and dry even in snow.

He had a small pack of emergency matches in a light plastic case, and a cable saw to cut wood for a fire or emergency shelter. Tucked in the pack was 200 feet of braided steel fishing line that was not any thicker than string, but it could lift a log or hold his weight if needed.

Jack could use his pack like a climbing harness with the steel cable in the event he had to climb up or down. The last, but most important item in the pack, was a lightweight ceramic knife.

He felt it was overkill to wear the pack for every run, but Jack promised his dad and Uncle Mick he would.

And he kept that promise. Even though Dad, Mom, and Uncle Mick were now gone, even though it seemed silly. It would feel weird to run at the cabin without the pack. Mick always told Jack training with the extra weight of the pack gave him an advantage in races when he was two pounds lighter. No matter because he had to wear it anyway.

Jack found Doc Mayo waiting on the sidewalk outside the dorm after his last trip upstairs. As he opened the car door, she glanced at her watch and smiled, "Two more minutes and I would have come looking for you with my taser."

4

They headed out of town, into the countryside. About forty-five minutes into the one-hour drive, Jack realized Doc Mayo had not asked him for directions, hadn't plugged in GPS, and didn't have a map. She might have looked at directions before they left, but still, it was weird because she was driving like she knew where to go.

As they headed toward the home Jack had not seen for two years, they talked about school and light conversational stuff. He was glad she did not try to shrink his head along the way. He was her captive in the car, and she could have grilled him.

The house still looked the same. It was obvious someone had been keeping the place up while he was hiding out at school. The lawn looked mowed, and everything was neat and tidy outside. In fact, it looked much neater than when his parents were living here. He really did not want to go inside that cold and lonely house. It would never be the same without his mom and dad there, and his younger sister running around inside. It was still hard to believe he had lost all his family and Mick in one fell swoop.

Jack thought back to his birthday that year. He had been on the track finishing a workout when Coach Sulli stopped him and asked him to come to her office. She looked really upset and was not talking. Jack wondered what could have happened. *What did I do now?* His season had been so much better than anyone could have predicted for a first-year student from a small-town high school. Since coming to the college, Jack had not lost one race in his first season in cross-country or track. He had set course records in cross-country. During the track season, he had broken national college records in the 1500m, mile, 5k, and 10k, a feat never before accomplished, let alone dreamed of. His future seemed magical, so what could it be that was on the coach's mind?

When they got to her office Coach Sulli opened the door and motioned him in, telling him to have a seat. Inside her office sat a solemn woman who Sulli introduced as Doctor Mayo.

It was Doc Mayo who spoke first. "Jack, we have some bad news for you. There's been an accident." Jack sat numb and frozen as she told him his parents, sister, and an unidentified man had died in a freak car accident while on their way to the college to see him.

Coach Sulli knew it was his nineteenth birthday and that his parents and sister were coming to the college to take him out for a celebration dinner. She wondered if the other man in the car was his uncle. Mick had met Sulli at the beginning of the year, and he had come to all his races.

Jack had sat in stunned silence at the news that his whole family was gone.

He came back to the present, he was at his family home and about to meet with a lawyer. God only knows what he wanted. He always said he hated lawyers as much as he did shrink doctors. They both always wanted to mess with your life.

Stepping through the open front door into his family's living room, Jack was flooded with memories of a happier time when he still had a family. Everything looked the same as it did the last time he was here. As he poked his head into the kitchen, he noticed the only thing missing was the mail on the kitchen table. The family rule was whoever picked up the daily mail had to put it on the kitchen table. No mail on this kitchen table. *There wouldn't be, would there? My family is gone.* As Jack stepped out of the kitchen and back into the family room, he saw a familiar face.

With a huge smile spreading across his face, Jack crossed the room to the man, enveloping him a big hug. "Jim, I haven't seen you in years! What brings you here? I thought I was going to meet with a lawyer."

At 5'10", Jack was average height for a runner, and Jim towered over Jack by at least a foot. He looked like he was seven feet tall. With a big grin and an even bigger voice, the man said, "Hello, Jack." Then he added with a grin, "I am the lawyer."

"What?"

"Yes, Jack, I really am a lawyer. Your father did not want you to know too much about what was happening. He let you think I was just a fun-loving schoolmate of your parents. I have been your parents' friend since grade school, that part is true. I have also been your dad's lawyer since he needed someone he could trust with legal matters. Before that, I was first Mick's lawyer."

Jim led Jack and Doc Mayo over to the dining room table that had once been the center of so many happy, noisy family meals. He said, "Jack, we have important things to discuss, but first, let me go over some things that will help make sense of what I am about to tell you.

"Like I told you, I am a lawyer. I am also from your Uncle Mick's tribe. I know you know a little of the story of Mick's tribe. You may not know that Doc Mayo here is also a member of our tribe. She went to work at the college after the accident, so we could keep an eye on you. I know that sounds weird, but we could not take the chance that something would happen to you. Your mother and father are also members of our tribe."

Stunned, Jack blurted out, "But I thought there were only one hundred members of Uncle Mick's tribe still alive, and they were all in hiding,"

"Yes, it is true, the national records indicate that." Jim's voice grew very serious as he continued. "The elders of the tribe knew something was not right years ago. They hid tribal members all over the world and changed tribal records so no one would know the real numbers. When the raiders came to the village to massacre the tribe, only a couple dozen were there. The doctored records showed they were the only members of the tribe left before the massacre. That was not too unusual for native tribes back then. Tribes just died out from issues of illness, abuse, and neglect.

"The real facts are the elders had hidden almost 160 members of the tribe in various locations. Your mother and father were among them, which is why they lived here. The national government believed all but one of the known tribal members had died in that raid. But that tribal member was out of the country at the time."

He stopped talking for a moment and just looked at Jack. Then he said, "That tribal member was your Uncle Mick. Their land remained in a trust until tribal members were contacted by the government. Today over five thousand tribal members are living around the world in hiding.

"We are hiding because there is still the worry our lives are in danger. If the US government or various business entities that stand to lose a great deal of money and land find out that we survived, they might want to kill us all."

"But why?" asked Jack, not comprehending.

"Let me save that answer for a bit later," said Jim. "For now, let me tell you some things you will need to know."

5

As Jim continued, Doc Mayo brought in some steaming cups of tea from the kitchen. The lawyer said, "What very few people in and out of the Native American tribes know is the treaties sometimes had an end date on them. Most treaties signed between 1700 and 1800 had a 200-year limit. The American government believed most natives would die out or integrate into the white race. It's true - tribes did disappear, and their records were lost or destroyed.

"Jack, our treaty time limit is up in twenty years. Our tribe is the last treaty remaining to expire. With Mick gone—the last tribal member as far as they know—the government thinks all the land will finally be theirs."

"Will it?" Jack asked.

Jim shook his head. He said the land signed over was only a loan. After the 200-year limit, the property would be returned to the tribes that had signed the treaty. The government did not worry about returning the land for the first hundred years. Dozens of the original tribes had disappeared, or the treaties had been renegotiated by 1900, so there was less for the government to worry about.

"Starting around 1900, the US government and exceptionally large companies which stood to lose money were beginning to worry.

Everyone could see there was going to be a problem, and the troubles for us began. They tried everything to get rid of the remaining Indian tribes with a 200-year loan agreement, but there were still too many of us who knew about the real treaty deadlines. They decided it was necessary to do something soon.

"For two decades, the government and businesses waged a silent and hidden war on the remaining Native American tribes who still had a treaty with the time limit. Tribes disappeared and tribes were dispersed by the government all over the United States. Tribal members went to prison and were forgotten. It was a grim time, but the tribes managed to survive and even grew, as ours did."

"Now, Jack," said Jim, "I am about to tell you the most shocking news of your life." Looking right at Jack with his blue eyes and white-blond hair, Jim said, "You were not adopted. You are your parents' biological child."

"What?" Jack said wide-eyed.

"Yes, Jack, they were your real family. When you were born, Mick knew something was special about you. Your light hair and blue eyes marked you as an incredibly special person."

Jack remembered Mick telling him stories years ago about the only blond-haired, blue-eyed member of his tribe who had been born many generations ago. No one really knew for sure when that was, but the story had been passed down for generations. Jack had always thought Mick had made up the story to make him feel better about being a blond-haired, blue-eyed white kid instead of a Native like Mick.

Jim looked at Jack and said, "Jack, it is true that the first chief and shaman of our tribe had white hair and eyes like a wolf. He was the father of our tribe thousands of years ago." He stopped talking and remarked, "By the look on your face, you are finding this hard to believe."

"This is all a little too much . . ." Jack replied in a shaky voice.

Jim spoke softly but firmly as he continued. "Lobo, listen to me carefully. You are destined to be the next shaman of our tribe. Tomorrow, everyone will know that you are your parents' true birth son. You are also Mick's nephew and closest relative. By *everyone*, I mean we will put out a news release announcing you are Mick's nephew and that you will be inheriting his entire estate, as well as your parents' estate."

Jack could no longer sit at the table quietly and began pacing the living room. "For real? I can't believe it."

"It's true, Jack," replied Jim. "We could not take a chance of the authorities finding out you were Mick's relative in the event he was identified by the government. Mick's identity must now have been discovered."

"How?" asked Jack.

"Just four weeks before the accident, underground reports were released, including an old picture showing Mick signing a treaty."

"So . . . ?" asked Jack.

"The picture was from 1834."

"No way," Jack said. "You can't expect me to believe that!"

"Yes, Jack. Mick was much older than he looked. Much older." After a pause, Jim said, "Mick was already over a hundred years old when he signed that treaty in 1834."

"Oh, come on now. Do you expect me to believe Uncle Mick was over 300 years old when he died?"

"Jack, I am over a hundred years old myself," Jim said calmly. "In fact, Doc Mayo is almost a hundred herself."

As Doc Mayo nodded in confirmation, Jack shouted, "Bull!"

"No, Jack, long life is an added benefit we get from being a member of Mick's tribe. We are the longest-living people on Earth."

Jack sat back down. "I can't believe it. Jim, are you really over a hundred years old?"

"I am," said Jim.

"And you said you were grade-school friends with my parents, right?

"Right."

"Then that means my parents were also over a hundred years old too."

"Yes, they were Jack." Jim sat down next to Jack and put his arm around him.

"Lobo, you do not know how long I have waited to tell you who you really are," Jim said. "I have wanted you to know how special you are, but Mick made me keep my mouth shut. As it turns out, he was right. If it were known you were related to Mick, you would have died as well. From what we have discovered, your parents and sister died just because they were with Mick. No one knew of their relationship, so their deaths were collateral damage.

"After tomorrow, when the world finds out you are a surviving tribe member, we will have to keep you out of sight until we can set up safety measures to protect you. Once we finalize the paperwork and declare to the government that you are indeed one of Mick's tribal members and the rightful inheritor of his entire estate, you should be safer. We'll have to produce copies of the treaty, of course."

Jack thought about inheriting from Uncle Mick, who didn't seem to own much except the café, and his parents, who had the modest family home and not much else. "So, what's the big deal with the inheritance? Is it worth fighting for?"

Jim looked at Jack and said, "Son, there's more to tell you. Much, much more."

6

"Lobo, we hold the title to hundreds of millions of acres of land in the United States, Mexico, Canada, and other places. We could take back our lands and kick everyone off them, but that would cause societal upheaval and perhaps outright war. We are working on a win-win solution for everyone."

"What was Mick's plan for handling the treaty?" asked Jack, gradually coming to terms with what he was hearing.

Jim paused for a few moments. "Mick was going to tell these governments they could keep the land they held, but they would have to pay a small rental fee to hold it. Let's just say it would be rent on a long-term agreement. I am sure they will see it is to their advantage to agree instead of having to give up much of Washington State and large tracts of land in other states and countries. The rental fee will be high, but only pennies on the millions—not so high that it will profoundly impact their financial resources.

"Once they feel reassured that we are not going to take back the land, you and the rest of the tribal members will be safe. The crux of the matter is that instead of paying rent right away, they will use the rent money—which amounts to billions—to clean up the world by using better manufacturing techniques, recycling, and adding more green energy, like wind and solar power. In effect, they will put that rent money into cleaning the environment."

Jim looked at Jack and said, "Lobo, you can expect to become even richer than you already are. Mick owns green businesses that will earn funds from teaching these governments, businesses, and individuals how to accomplish this."

Jack stared blankly when he asked, "Did you just say *billions* of dollars?"

"Yes, I did, Lobo. Do you have any idea of the amount of money Mick and your parents left you?"

"Not a clue," said Jack, "but I do know they had enough to send me to college."

Jim laughed and said, "They sure did. Jack, I have been helping Uncle Mick and your parents for decades. Living a long life means you can amass a huge fortune if you are wise. Uncle Mick had been buying land for over a hundred years. He has hidden corporations that have bought up much of the free land in Washington State and beyond. He owns the land surrounding Mt. Rainier that is not part of the Mt. Rainier National Park."

Jim looked at Jack for a moment, "Mick told me once that land around Mt. Rainier is the most sacred land to our tribe and needed to belong to the tribe.

"Mick's proposal also includes having the remaining property around Mt. Rainier given back to the tribe, including Mt. Rainier itself. Since Mt. Rainier is a national park, it will not be too hard to get the US government to agree to it because they do not have to let the public know.

"The tribe will still allow visitors into the park as normal. The more remote areas near Mick's cabin will be off-limits to the public. People seldom hike those areas anyway, so it will not cause too much of a problem."

"But where do the billions come in?" asked Jack.

"Let's just say with what your Uncle Mick was worth, he could buy Gates, Musk, and Bezos one hundred times over. The money, property, and business are so well hidden that no one outside our group knows what he owns. I usually just say, 'Mick is well off.'"

Realizing that all this must be a quantum leap for Jack, Jim said, "Sorry for dumping all this on you at once. I know it must be a shock."

"Shock, alright. My head is spinning. I'm heading up to the cabin today to train. I need some time alone. But I sure didn't expect to hear all this."

"Perfect," said Jim. "I already anticipated that. Lobo, you'll need to keep out of the public eye for a while. If you stay there for the next few months, I should be able to get things set up with the authorities to ensure your safety."

Should, Jim thought, *should?* He knew his life would never be the same after what he had just heard.

Jack told Jim and Doc Mayo, "Life as I know it began at Mick's cabin, and I need to go back to regain my balance. Do what you have to do with all the paperwork and advise me when you need to. This has been a big day for me, and I don't mean because I turned twenty-one."

Jim smiled at Jack's words. "Don't worry, Lobo. No one knows about Mick's cabin, so it should be safe and quiet. I will keep the press off your back. Go on up to the cabin and get used to your new reality."

Doc Mayo went into the kitchen and came out with a small chocolate birthday cake and cut everyone generous pieces while they all sang an off-key "Happy Birthday" to him.

Jim said, "Oh, and you don't know this, but Mick had me do some nice improvements to the place since your last visit two years ago."

"Like what?" Jack was looking forward to finding the cabin of his childhood memories just as he had left it and wasn't sure if he liked the idea of too many changes.

"Well, Mick had a plan I was to put in motion in the event of his death. I did everything he asked, but I like surprises, so you will have to wait to see the changes until after you get to the cabin."

"Thanks, Jim, I guess." Jack turned to Doc Mayo, "Can't believe after these two years of you trying to shrink my head, you turn out to be a relative—and an old one at that." He let out a laugh.

Doc Mayo laughed. She said, "I may be an old lady, but I can still turn a head or two."

Jack's cheeks turned red because he realized Doc must have known he had a little crush on her. She also knew about Michelle and how Jack felt about her. For the past two years, she had tried talking Jack into at least calling Michelle.

Jim produced paperwork for Jack to sign, and when they were done, he and Doc Mayo prepared to leave.

As everyone said their goodbyes at the door, Jim said, "Jack, I know this has been a lot, but it had to be done today. Mick instructed us to wait until you were twenty-one before putting all this into play. The press is going to have a heyday with all this information, and the government is really going to take a flying spin over the news.

"The plan is to schedule my announcement to appear on the 5:00 o'clock news tomorrow night. I think it would be best for you to be up at the cabin by then. If not, things could get a bit hairy around here for you unless you'd enjoy news crews lined up around the block and around the clock . . . you being the new rich kid on the block and all."

"I get your drift, Jim," said Jack with a stunned look on his face." I'll get on the road by early morning."

"I'll contact you if I need to. Remember, Lobo, no one knows about the cabin, so you should have privacy until you return to school in the fall. You are planning to go back to college, aren't you?"

"Why wouldn't I?" Jack asked.

"Oh, I thought you might think you don't need a degree now that you are rich."

"I may not need school to earn a good living now, but I really need to run, so I am going back."

He hugged Doc Mayo and said, "Hey Doc, tell Coach Sulli I am doing well, and she should plan on me breaking records next season. Tell her I said she may have to expand her trophy case."

Doc Mayo grinned. "Will do, Lobo."

Jim said, "One more thing. Do not take your cell phone with you.

Pull the battery from your phone first thing in the morning after you make any calls you may need to make and place the phone and battery on the kitchen counter."

"Why?"

"Well, Jack, unless you want everyone, their brother, the press, and the government finding you, you need to leave it here."

"Oh, my God, you are right! Makes me want to give my phone to someone about to board a cruise ship. See you soon!"

After Jim and Doc Mayo left, Jack walked around his old home. For a small house, it sure seemed big and quiet when he was alone. Walking into his old bedroom, he saw it was exactly as he had left it two years earlier. The only difference was that someone had hung the awards he had won over the last two years on the wall like his mom would have. His mom couldn't have hung them, but whoever did must have known his mom well. She always hung his awards even though Jack did not care about them.

His mother always made him feel proud of his achievements. He would say, "Oh, Mom, they're no big deal."

She would softly tap his shoulder and say, "They are too." Afterward, she would make him something wonderful to eat, and the world seemed better.

It really hurt to lose her. Now that he knew she had given birth to him, and they were flesh and blood, her loss hurt even deeper. He had always appreciated and loved his family, but there was always that bit of insecurity about being adopted. Now his love for them welled up because of their sacrifices to keep him safe.

Stop feeling sorry for yourself, he told himself later as he took a prepared meal out of the fridge, heated it up and sat down to eat it alone at the big family dining room table. He had a job to do and goals to accomplish. He knew he needed to finish the next year strong and be there for his extended family. He thought about the many relatives he had never known about and realized his dream of being Native had come true. His whole life, he had wanted to belong in the tribe, and now he really was family.

7

When Jack awoke in the morning, he felt as if he were a different person. Before he even got out of bed, the weight of the new responsibilities that came with being a future shaman and leader of his new extended tribal family descended on him. Determined not to stress about it, he figured it just meant his life would be a bit fuller than he had planned.

Doc Mayo had told him they had stocked the house, and Jack found plenty he could take with him to the cabin. Doc had removed anything that could spoil but left him ingredients for a good breakfast. After he had eaten, Jack cleaned up and packed up the food supplies and things he would need for his three months in hiding.

Jim had said the cabin was remodeled. Jack was not sure what that meant but hoped it meant hot water. Mick used to say, "There's nothing like a cold shower after a hard run." Mick was usually right, but Jack was still convinced that a hot shower felt great on a chilly morning. As he loaded his gear into his truck, Jack wondered if the cabin had a TV. Probably not. Mick hated TV and thought it was the perfect way to suck a brain empty. Mick was a book man.

By 8:00 a.m., he had the truck loaded and was headed in heavy traffic out of Bellevue to the south side of Mt. Rainier. Wonderful memories of time spent with Mick at the cabin ran through Jack's head as he drove.

Three hours later, Jack arrived in the tiny town of Cougar Ridge, where Uncle Mick's house was tucked away behind his café. The sign above the square white building said Last Stop Café, but the locals had always referred to it as *the* café, probably because it was the only one for miles. Cougar Ridge was small, with only a gas station, the Last Stop café, a small grocery store, and a tiny post office.

Jack stepped out of the truck, smelled the unmistakable scent of pine and cedar and stretched. He looked at the café at the end of the driveway and it looked like it was open. His thoughts immediately went to Michelle. The last time he had seen her, she was working there as a short-order cook. Would she still be working here? She probably hadn't stayed on after Mick's death.

It was so messed up that he hadn't even called or come to see her even once. But he had his own troubles, thinking of the black hole of grief he had dropped into after his family had been killed.

His stomach rumbled, and he thought he'd get something to eat. That would give him an excuse to see if Michelle was still there. He wondered if she'd be mad at him. He knew he was taking a chance on the town regulars recognizing him. But hunger took precedence over his plans to keep a low profile and propelled him to the entrance.

When Jack walked in the door of the café, he did not see Michelle or anyone else for that matter. The red booths, gingham-checked half curtains at the windows, and the rustic décor on the walls looked the same. The place still looked the same as the last time he was here. In fact, it looked the same as it had the first day he walked into this place eighteen years earlier.

When no one appeared, he called out, "Hi, are you open for lunch?" As he waited for an answer, Jack looked around. He had not heard an answer to his call, so he called out once more. "Hello, is this place open for lunch yet?"

"Be right there. Have a seat!" The voice coming from the kitchen sounded impatient. He'd know that voice anywhere.

What a jerk you are . . . you stroll back into this place after over two years, demanding a meal without so much as a "Hi Michelle" or "I'm sorry, Michelle." No, the big dumb jock just struts on in and demands a meal.

Jack spun around and his eyes fell on Michelle, beautiful as always with her striking green eyes and long dark hair. Fleeting thoughts rushed in of all the times he had come into the café looking for food but really only to see Michelle.

They had always had so much fun, running the trails together and teasing each other. Michelle was a natural runner but was not into competition. When he first met her, she could outrun him. Of course, she was seventeen, and he was just twelve. It was close, but she beat him and never let him forget it. By the next year, he could have beaten her, but they always ran for fun after that first race.

"Is that you, Jack? Has all that running made you mute? Did you forget how to talk, or don't you remember me?" Michelle's bright eyes twinkled and her mouth curved in a wide smile.

With a start, Jack came back to the present and said, "Hi, Michelle," in a quiet voice.

"Hi? Is that all you can say after you made me wait two years for you to show up," she shot back, her smile broadening. "Yes, the running took his brain. Ah, don't worry, Jack. I'm just teasing you. I knew you had to work things out for yourself before you could manage coming back to this place again. Although a letter or even a call would have been nice . . ."

"Michelle, I am so sorry. Please forgive me for not contacting you."

"I already have," she said, walking toward him. "Now, come here and give me a hug."

Jack did not need any prodding. He took three large strides and wrapped his long arms around her. Michelle was as tall as Jack, and she fit into his arms perfectly. He looked into Michelle's eyes and smiled. "I don't know why I couldn't come to see you. My head's been messed up. Maybe it's because I lost everyone close to me and did not want to take a chance that you would leave too."

"Oh, Jack, I will never leave you. I have been your friend for too many years to leave. I'll admit the wait was hard, and there were times I wanted to see you, but I knew you would be in touch in your own time. You had a lot of pain to work through."

"And now more stuff to work through," said Jack.

"What do you mean? What's happened now?"

"I'll tell you all of it later. Let's just say a ton of bricks came down on me yesterday."

"Oh, yah. It was your 21st birthday."

"You remembered."

As Jack hugged Michelle, he had the strangest sensation that he was reading her thoughts and she was reading his. At that moment, he knew she felt the same about him as he felt for her.

He felt as if he were floating. He had never held Michelle before except for a quick hug or when they play wrestled when he was years younger. Jack heard another sigh from Michelle and pulled her even tighter.

Memories of their time spent together ran through his mind. He remembered all those times he would sneak looks at her while she worked in the kitchen. He thought of their five-year age difference and how it was so important when he was twelve. Now that he was twenty-one and she was twenty-six, it didn't seem to matter.

"Too tight?" he asked. He knew Michelle was not fighting to get out of this hug.

"No way, you silly fool, I lost you for two years, and I don't want to lose you again."

"Don't worry, Michelle. I am not going back to school for four months. I came back here to train and get my life back together."

"Good to hear, Jack. I would hate to have to tie you up in the storeroom just so I can keep you around."

They both laughed, and Michelle hugged him even tighter before stepping back.

They stood and talked for a while until Jack started hearing a faint sound of people murmuring. Jack looked up to see that a crowd had assembled at the door.

A voice called out, "So, are you two love birds going to stand there all day, or can we get some lunch?"

Jack took his eyes off Michelle momentarily and saw half a dozen people were watching them. The lunch crowd had arrived.

"How did you get in here without us noticing?" Michelle asked.

"Without you noticing?' said Bear, a tall, rugged man. "Hell, we could have starved waiting for you two to break it up. We saw you were . . . ah . . . busy, so we waited outside. Then we came on in to see if you'd notice. Well, whatever, I'm hungry," said Bear. "I would really like to eat if you two lovebirds don't mind."

Michelle looked at the crowd, then at the clock, and then looked at Jack and laughed. "Looks like you are going to have to help me with lunch. That is if you can still cook after all these years?"

"Yes, I can still cook, or at least I think so," Jack said with a grin as he followed Michelle into the kitchen.

So much for me getting out of town before being seen, thought Jack.

"Hey, Lobo."

"Yeah?" said Jack looking at Bear.

"Wash those hands before you touch my food, will you?"

Jack reddened and ducked into the kitchen. There was a chorus of laughter as Jack went to wash up. Jack remembered working in this kitchen with Mick and Michelle. He learned all he knew about cooking from them.

Michelle was a teenager when she showed up at the café looking very hungry and with no money. She had hitchhiked from New York, and her last ride had stopped in Cougar Ridge for gas. While the driver was filling the tank, Michelle went inside to use the restroom. When she returned to the pump, her ride was gone, and her backpack and all her money went with him.

She wandered into the café and asked Mick if she could wash dishes for a meal. Mick listened to her story, then served her up a huge meal. When she was done, he showed her the kitchen sink, where she paid her tab elbow-deep in the soapy water.

Michelle had been in and out of foster homes all her life. She didn't remember her real parents. When she was older, she learned that she had been left on the steps of a fire station as a baby. The firefighters turned her over to the authorities, and for the next seventeen years, she surfed the foster system. When she turned seventeen, and with nothing to keep her in New York, Michelle set out to see the country by thumb.

"That's not a smart thing to do for a seventeen-year-old girl," Mick had told her.

"I realize that now," she had replied.

Mick had an extra bunkroom in the back of the café, and he offered it to her for the night, and she accepted. When Mick arrived at the restaurant in the morning to get things ready for breakfast, he found all the lights on. He was sure he had turned everything off and stepped in with caution. And then he smelled the coffee and bacon.

"I was wondering when you would show up," Michelle said, coming out of the kitchen. "I made you some breakfast." Mick started to speak, but Michelle cut him off, saying, "You're going to need a good breakfast if you're going to be able to work hard all day." Mick wisely shut his mouth and sat down fast because everything smelled so good.

Mick's first bite of her fluffy omelet and crispy home fries brought a huge smile to his face.

He didn't say a word until his plate was clean. Then the first words out of his mouth were, "You're hired if you would like to stay on and cook."

Michelle gladly accepted. That was nine years earlier, and she was still there.

Michelle began calling out orders for Jack to cook. Bear called out, too, to ask if Jack's hands had been washed.

Jack heard Michelle tell Bear, "If you ever want to eat here again, you'd better keep your yap shut." Jack had known Bear his whole life and knew Bear was a good guy and a big joker. He also expected that Bear was one of Mick's tribal members, which made Bear a member of his tribe as well.

Jack immediately noticed the greasy, typical diner food choices from years ago had changed. The menu offerings were now all healthy —healthy breads, bacon without nitrates, organic eggs, and plenty of fruits and vegetables. Jack wondered when those changes had been made and if the patrons liked the changes. At least, their bodies are better off for it, he was sure of that.When Jack came out of the kitchen, Bear asked him, "How long are you planning on being in town?"

"I'm here for the summer. But, hey, you need to keep it quiet about me being here." Jack looked around the room at dark heads bent over their meals or joking and talking with their neighbors.

"No worries, Jack," Bear said. "Everyone here today is a tribal member. It's safe to talk." The only one Bear didn't know about was Michelle, but Mick had told him there was nothing Michelle could not know because Mick fully trusted her with his life.

"Hang on, Bear, don't leave yet. I need to talk to you and the others."

The noon rush was over, and Michelle said they would clean up later. She and Jack sat down at a big table and asked the others to gather around.

Knowing it would be on the news in just hours, Jack wanted to let everyone know what would be announced before they heard it from the media.

"Yesterday, I got some big news," he started, looking around at the curious faces surrounding him. "It was my twenty-first birthday, and I met with my family's lawyer, Jim. You know how we all thought I was adopted? Well, I found out yesterday that I am my parents' blood son. I wasn't adopted."

As murmurs started around the room, Jack motioned for quiet and continued. "Mick was my blood uncle, and I just found out I am his heir."

It was as if all the oxygen had been sucked out of the room. All eyes were on Jack as the listeners in the room digested what he had just said.

"An announcement will be made today that I will inherit all his holdings. You can understand why I don't want everyone to know I am here."

Jack looked around the room at who he now knew was all part of his large extended family—his tribe. Those words held a feeling of belonging and security for him that he had never known before.

Before everyone scattered, they assured him they would keep his whereabouts quiet from any outsiders or non-tribal members.

As he and Michelle began to clean up the lunch dishes, she asked Jack to tell her more about his stunning news. Jack told her the entire story as they worked but left out the part about Mick's real age. He also glossed over the massacres, and Mick's and his parents' deaths, so she would not worry about him. Michelle was wide-eyed when he finished.

"Why did your parents tell you that you were adopted?" she asked. "It was a cruel thing for your parents to hide from you the fact that they were your real parents. Your parents should have told you sooner."

"It was for my safety, Michelle." If they had not kept that from me and the rest of the world, I might have been in the car the day of the accident."

"Please don't talk like that, Jack. I don't think I could have survived if you had died too. Losing Mick was so hard on me. He had been like a father to me for those seven years. Life has been hard with him gone and not being able to see you these past two years."

Her green eyes misting with tears, Michelle said, "Jack, I am so glad you are back."

When they finished in the kitchen, Michelle wanted to show Jack Mick's house. There she told him Mick had turned over running the café to her years ago. After his death, she found he had left both the business and the house for her to use for the rest of her life. She never had to pay rent or worry about making a profit because he also left her enough funds to maintain everything. "I'm not wealthy by any means, but I don't have to work all the time if I don't want to."

Michelle looked around at Mick's comfortable house that she had now made her own and said, "This is home. My customers are my friends and my family." Laughing, she added, "I told all my customers I would cook only healthy because I care about them." Michelle could make dried-up old wood taste great, so none of her customers cared. They spent the rest of the afternoon catching up and then just enjoyed sitting together quietly.

After a while, Michelle broke the silence. "What time do you have to leave?"

"Oh, no time in particular. Why?"

"I was wondering if you want to stay the night, Michelle said. "And no, I am not making a move on you, but I don't want to say goodbye so quickly. We still have catching up to do, and we could have dinner. By then it will be late, so you can stay here if you want. You can sleep in your old room. Don't look so scared, Jack," she said, laughing at the look on his face.

Jack chuckled and said, "You don't scare me, Michelle. I would love to stay the night. By the way, what's for dinner?"

"Just like a college boy. All you think about is food."

"Hey, I think about running too."

"You are such a boy!"

They had both skipped lunch and realized they were starving, so Michelle pulled out some steaks, and Jack barbecued them while she put together a big salad. They ate in the cozy kitchen because it was still too cool at night to eat on the back porch. After dinner, they sat on the sofa talking. As Jack put his arm around Michelle, and she snuggled in closer, he had the feeling that he had come home - just where he needed to be.

One minute they were talking, the next thing Jack noticed was the pale morning light coming through the window. They had both fallen asleep together on the sofa.

It was Sunday morning, and Michelle told Jack she didn't have to be at the restaurant until 9:00 to get ready for brunch, so they had time for coffee and a roll. Both were quiet as they sipped their coffee.

Jack knew leaving would be hard, but they both knew he had to. Without his family, his friendship with Michelle was all that he had. They held hands as they slowly walked to the truck.

As Jack drove away from the café, he could see Michelle waving in the rearview mirror. It would be a long week until he saw her again.

8

The turn-off to the road to the cabin was only blocks away from the café and was marked with a small sign nailed to a large stump. If Jack had been driving faster than the five miles per hour he was going, he would have missed it. The road to the cabin was only four miles from the main road, and it was in better shape than other graveled roads in the area, but he still took it slow.

He passed the old farm down the road that had been abandoned for decades. With no other cabins on the road, it would be a rarity for a car to make it as far as Mick's cabin considering there were "Private Property/Keep Out" signs all the way up the dirt road.

As he pulled up into the driveway, Jack began to get his first feeling of the solitude he would be dealing with that summer. He knew Michelle wouldn't be that far away, but with no other signs of civilization around him, it somehow felt more remote.

The drive up the private road had only taken him twenty minutes. Jack knew the eight miles into town and back would be an easy long run. He figured it would be an easy midday run to head into town, see Michelle, eat lunch, and return to the cabin.

As Jack reached the cabin and pulled into the driveway, he was glad to see it still looked the same as it had the first time he had seen it so many years ago. Jack inserted the key and opened the door to see the familiar open room and a loft with a sitting area, kitchen, and a small sleeping area where Mick used to sleep. The sleeping area had a bed and a small dresser. The sitting area had a small sofa and comfortable chairs. No TV. Jack knew the only thing electrical in this cabin had been a battery-operated radio. When Jack tried the radio, he found the battery to be dead. He figured that gave him his first excuse to go back into town.

He walked through the kitchen area, unlocked the back door, and stepped into what had been the back porch, now completely enclosed with no windows. With the light from the kitchen revealing light fixtures and switches, he knew the cabin had electricity. Locating a switch, he flicked on a light above the door.

The light revealed bookcases full of books, filing cabinets, and even a desk with what looked like a state-of-the-art computer sitting on it. Jack was blown away because Mick always said he hated technology, so why all the changes now? Noticing a note taped to the computer screen, Jack saw it was from Jim, his lawyer. It read:

> *Jack, Mick always knew there was a chance he would be found out and killed, so he made plans for things to continue without him. Everything you need to know is on this computer. Place your palm on the reader next to the keyboard. Failure to do so will destroy the computer's memory irretrievably. Good luck with finding out everything you want and need to learn.*

Jack slumped into the desk chair and sighed. Memories of his family tore at his heart like scar tissue breaking open. After a long hesitation, Jack moved his hand above the reader and then slowly set his hand down on the surface. As soon as his palm touched the reader, lights started blinking, and the screen flickered to life with an image of his beloved Uncle Mick staring back at him. Then he heard Mick's voice.

"Hi, my little Lobo. First, I am sorry that your life has been turned upside down by what has happened. If you are hearing this message, then the worst has happened. Not only have I been killed, but so have your mother, father, and your little sister. There is no way I can reach out to comfort you, but I will try to help you make sense of the confusion you must be feeling at this moment."

Tears streaked down Jack's face as he listened to the man who had been so important in his life and realized again the depth of his loss.

"Let me first explain that for twenty-one years, I have been making recordings for every eventuality in the event of my demise and the possible loss of your family. As cold as what I had to do sounds, it had to be done to protect you and the rest of our tribe.

"This video is just one of thousands I have made for you. Some are not relevant and will not be played. Recordings will be played in the future, but only as you need them. I must ask you to trust me and be patient. I am giving you information as needed, not just when you want it. If I were to give you all the information right now, it would ruin everything we have planned for centuries.

"To access the proper information, you must also ask the correct questions. Because you are watching this video, I know you have just turned twenty-one, and it is the summer before your senior year in college. I am sure Jim has explained much to you, but I know you also have questions. I promise you I will answer all of them in time.

"I warn you that you have work to do before you are ready to learn everything. The most important thing is you must look forward in life. Make sure our deaths are not in vain. You have a responsibility to yourself, your family, and now as you know, to your tribe.

"I understand the pressure of the expectations that will be placed on you will be heavy, but you can manage it. You have what it takes to fulfill your destiny as the leader of our people.

"I assume you have questions you would like answers for. Now is the time to ask. This computer is a bit more advanced than any you have come across in that old college you have been attending," Mick said, flashing his big familiar Mick smile.

"I have recorded thousands of messages to you and added more data that you will need in the future. For now, it is question-and-answer time.

"There are limits to what I am going to reveal to you at this time, but I want you to ask any question you have, and I will answer if I can. When you want to ask a question, start with "Uncle Mick, I have a question." Mick fell silent then, and the image on the screen froze after his last word.

Jack had been sitting on the edge of his seat with his mouth open, and now he slumped back in the chair and exhaled deeply. He was not sure how long he had sat motionless, but it felt like an hour had passed before he could move. All the while, Mick's face stayed frozen on the screen before him.

Is this real? Can I really ask this man who is no longer alive questions?

"Uncle Mick, I have a question," he said in a voice that wasn't quite steady. "How old are you?"

Mick's picture flickered, and a differently dressed Mick appeared on the screen. "I thought you would ask that one, Lobo. You were always the one who had a tough time believing what you were told. The truth is I am not sure exactly how old I am. I know for sure I'm over 300 years old. It was in the 1700s when I first saw a white man's calendar. As far as how much older than that I am, I'm not sure. Just say I made it to over 300. I did not run too bad for an old man, did I? The image of Mick laughed heartily. "Do not feel bad that it took you until you were fifteen before you could outrun me. With luck, you will live much longer than I did."

Mick's face again froze on the screen. Jack leaned back in his chair. How could it be true that Mick was older than three hundred? The thought of living to be that old made Jack sit quietly for a while before he could ask another question.

"Uncle Mick, I have a question. Am I really my parents' birth son?"

Mick's picture again changed a bit before he spoke again. "It is true. They are your real parents. My dear Lobo, not telling you about your true birthright was the hardest thing your parents and I ever had to do. They were both working to prepare things for the 200th anniversary when your mother became pregnant. It was not planned, but they were so happy, as was I.

"The shock came with your birth. Thankfully, they were in a Native American clinic when you were born. You arrived with pure white hair and those white, blue eyes you are known for. Genetically, it should have been an impossibility as both of your parents were dark-haired Natives. In fact, your father probably wondered if your mother had fooled around. Had I not been around, there might have been a bit of trouble. When I saw you, I knew who and what you were."

Jack got up from his chair, went into the kitchen and paced around, thinking about what it must have been like for his parents to be faced with a Caucasian-appearing newborn. Undoubtedly, that made it easier for them to pass him off as adopted to protect him.

Who Jack had always thought he had been was a lie. He felt deeply shaken by what he was learning. He shook his head, trying to put all the pieces together. It was a lot to handle.

After he had settled back in his chair, he got curious about the family and tribe he had been born into, and he said once again, "Uncle Mick, I have a question. What is the history of our tribe?"

Once again, Uncle Mick appeared in a different but familiar plaid pearl-buttoned shirt. He began to speak. "Thousands of years ago, our people came to this land now called Washington State. It was many years before the white man discovered the new world. The white man was still in what we now call Europe. Our people landed on the shores of this continent 1,000 generations ago. The best I can figure out is that it was over 20,000 years ago. They settled on the shores of what is now called Puget Sound.

"In the distance, they saw a mountain of the gods, which the white man now calls Mt. Rainier. For generations, our people were afraid to go near it for fear of angering the gods, but we were always drawn to it.

"But it was the birth of the one who we call the 'Great Father' that changed everything.

When the Great Father was born, our tribe changed forever. Like you, he was born with white hair and light-blue eyes.

"Yes, Lobo, you are the second of our people born with white hair and blue eyes, which is why I took such pains to hide you from the world. Our people sent messages to every tribe to announce the Great Father's birth. No one knew his significance, but all knew it was a sign.

"As he grew older, The Great Father's wisdom became apparent. Even as a young child, he understood things that our people had questions about. For years, he traveled the lands, teaching wonderful things to all the tribes. We prospered and lived a peaceful existence in which war was non-existent.

"Then came the time the Great Father said we must travel to the sacred mountain that is now called Rainier. Only the bravest would travel with him. They set out on a trip from which all wondered if they would return, that is, all except for the Great Father. It was as though he knew something was there for him and traveling to the mountain was his destiny.

"After they reached the mountain, it took days for them to find the land you are on now. The Great Father seemed to be guided by a spirit. He led them up through the pass into the crater in which you and I used to run. When they saw the lake, the island, and sheer cliffs, they believed they had reached the land of the gods. The Great Father could not get them to go further than the shoreline of the lake. He told them to camp while he explored the land beyond.

"The men set up camp while the Great Father walked ahead alone. The men heard strange and alien noises they had never heard before and wanted to run away, but they stayed at the shore as the Great Father had asked.

"It was a frightening time for them before the Great Father returned. He returned to their camp carrying a spear with a shiny glowing point. As he charged them with the task, the Great Father explained, 'This spear is a sign that our people must move here and become the guardians of the lake. This place is sacred. No man must defile it. We are the chosen ones.'

"All but two of the men returned to their village with news of what they had found. They were to divide the tribe in two. Half were to stay in the village, and the other half were to return to build a new village below the lake.

"That village is now our town—Cougar Ridge—where my house and the café are. Yes, Lobo, our people have been at that site for twenty thousand years."

Jack was awestruck by what Mick had said. He had studied anthropology and knew no sign of man had been found in this area before 12,000 BC. Mick must be wrong, or the old tales were off. As if Mick's recording could read his mind and he answered his question.

"Lobo, I know, with your education, you are thinking I am wrong about the dates. I have checked them myself. An unexplained ice age at about 12,000 BC killed off all the people who were here before that time. Only our village here by the mountain was spared as the 14,000-foot height of the mountain and the shape of the crater protected them. Millions perished in the thousand-year ice age that followed. I cannot say more about how they survived at this time, but when you ask the correct question, I will reveal more." "Lobo, you have a great history behind you. You have much to learn. It is true you are your parents' natural-born son, and you are of my blood. As the second of our people born with the sign of white hair and light blue eyes, you also have been given a great responsibility. I am sorry to burden you so greatly, but your people need you. You will learn and discover a great deal about life in the future, but for now, you must prepare yourself to lead.

"The first matter at hand is the preparation of your body if you are to live long as I did. Yes, Lobo, you can live as long as I did and longer, but you must be healthy and smart to do so. I suggest you take a break from the computer now and eat if needed. Then you need to get back to your training. By training, I mean you need to go to the crater and run.

"I understand that since the loss of your family, you may not feel like a whole person. I expect you would not run as well as you could have due to the trauma and grief. But now, it is time to resume your training and live again so that those of us who gave our lives can live again through you.

"Jack, when you need to ask more questions, return and ask. Also, you will find everything you need for your studies in this room. This computer has access to any database you need, and I do mean *any* database. I have a feeling if you learn what I expect you to, you will need the access. Now, go on and settle in. You have work ahead of you."

With Mick's final words, the screen went blank, and the rest of the room went silent. Jack sat in the dim light for quite a while before he got up and left the room. He walked into the kitchen, looking around at the familiar kitchen area. It was simple, with a wood stove, sink with a hand pump, open shelves, and an old propane fridge. The wood stove was still the only source of heat for the cabin. He could see he would be getting good exercise by chopping wood. The nights were still cold, so he needed to make a fire to stay comfortable and do his cooking. He had seen a good stack of firewood as he drove up, so that would not be a problem. And there surely would be an ax or a saw. Mick seemed to have thought of everything.

The loft held two single beds. With the nights still cold, sleeping up in the loft would be warmer, so Jack unloaded his sleeping bag onto one of the beds.

By now, it was a little after three in the afternoon when Jack went outside to bring in some wood. The old outhouse was in its place with the proverbial half-moon on the door as an example of Mick's sense of humor. Jack didn't look forward to stumbling outside to use the outhouse on dark nights and cold mornings.

He hauled in an armload of wood, happy to find it was dry and ready to burn, and then moved the rest of his gear into the cabin. He built a fire in the woodstove to heat the place up. In half an hour, the stove had heated the small cabin. Digging out a cast-iron frying pan Jack fried a large steak and heated canned beans. He threw together a green salad and ate it at the worn kitchen table.

When he finished dinner, he walked out on the covered porch on the front of the cabin. The bird and chipmunk sounds had quietened. All Jack could hear was the soothing sound of the river. He knew he would sleep well that night.

Inside, Jack grabbed a couple of extra blankets and headed upstairs. He barely remembered his head hitting the pillow before he fell into a deep sleep.

9

His sleep was deep and restful until early dawn when the sound of birds making a loud racket woke him. Sleep now over, he went out on the front porch to find a pair of blue jays keeping a sentinel watch.

He dressed for running, ate a light breakfast, threw energy bars and water into his pack, and headed up the main trail toward the lake. The run up toward the mountain was stunning, with huge old-growth trees big as redwoods alongside the trail. The river was wide here and loud as he ran at an easy pace along the trail.

On this first run on the mountain in two years, he was reminded how fantastic it was up here in the mountains.

The trail was not too steep, which made running easy, and followed the main river for about four miles to the lake shore. Mick said the trail to the lake should always be used as the warmup and cool-down part of the run. The realization that Mick and he would never run this trail together again brought Jack to tears. Then he thought, *But, if what Mick says is true, I might be running here for over a hundred years!* Time had a different meaning now that he knew how old Mick had been.

At the lakeshore with its clear blue water, and green forest and majestic snow-capped mountain behind, he stopped and remembered how Mick said his tribe had come here for thousands of years to get closer to the spirit of the mountain.

He thought about how each shaman of his tribe before him had no doubt run this trail to become one with nature and his world.

The lower lake trail was perfectly flat, exactly three miles long, and perfect for doing fast tempo runs or two laps for a great fast 10K. The upper trail was tough—six miles long and had up and downhill stretches. To Jack, it felt harder than any 10K cross-country course in existence. Perfect for getting him ready for the upcoming season.

The upper trail had a feature he really liked. At one point, it came down a steep hill and went across a huge log onto the island in the middle of the lake, across another huge log, and up the other side. He knew he could build up speed going down, fly across the island, and push up the other side.

There were two one-mile-long uphill stretches where he could gain one thousand feet on each section. The one-mile run back down was blindingly fast and would allow him to catch just a bit of a breather before he had to climb back up another 1,000 feet. The trail was hard but beautiful beyond comparison. He knew he needed to regain his mountain legs to run those hills. Today he would only walk and jog.

The lake looked so inviting, Jack thought he'd rather clean up in the warmer lake, rather than the freezing river by the cabin. This area never had too much snow, so the lake was never too cold. Mick said the shape of the big mountain on the other side of the ridge protected this old crater from snow. He also said there was a geothermal vent under the lake that warmed it, so it was always nice to swim in, then he would dry off with a slow jog back to the cabin.

Jack removed his pack, stripped off his clothes, and walked over to the jumping rocks. Mick said when Jack was four years old, he had given the large boulders their name. Before jumping in, he checked the deep clear water for new logs or other obstructions and then dove off a rock into the lake. As always, swimming in the lake lifted his spirits.

Jack swam over to the island and began swimming around it. Mick used to have him swim in the lake to add cross-training to his workouts. It was probably his way to get him to bathe more often.

Everything seemed peaceful and quiet, but when he swam under the first log, he saw something moving in the bushes. Stopping, he floated and listened. He did not hear or see anything and continued swimming. This part of the forest had always been quiet. There were not many deer, bears, or even birds near the lake. Mick used to tell him it was because the forest animals knew this was sacred land and showed respect by staying away. Still, there were those times Jack was sure he had heard the sound of something following him in the woods when he ran.

While they were up in the crater, Mick used to tell him, "It's the sound of your guardian spirit protecting you while you run." The first time Jack heard about his guardian was on his seventh birthday. Mick had taken him to the crater to do his first-ever run around the lake. He had said, "Seven is the age of testing. Jack, if you are fit enough, you will receive a guardian spirit while you run around the lake."

That day he had to choose the three-mile flat loop or the six-mile hill course. He had been running in the forest by the cabin with Mick since he was four, so he decided to run the full six miles in hopes of impressing Uncle Mick. Jack ran the six-mile loop alone, and that was the first time he heard something in the trees. When Jack told Mick he heard something in the woods following him, the smile on Mick's face widened—the biggest smile Jack would ever see him smile.

Mick said, "It looks like a guardian decided to choose you, Lobo."

"What do you mean?"

"All who want to run here must have a guardian."

No matter how often he asked, Mick would just repeat, "It is a guardian."

From then on, Jack was allowed to run in the crater. In the beginning, he always ran the trails silently with Mick. But by the time he was twelve years old, Jack could run every trail alone if he carried his safety backpack.

But this day he was not running when he heard the noise. Jack was the first person in the crater in over two years. Whatever it was must have been surprised there was someone in it again.

It's just a deer, Jack thought, *no matter what Mick said*. A lonely deer was curious and probably wanted to see who was dumb enough to run lap after lap around a lake. As he continued his swim around the island, he couldn't help wondering if it was something else he had always heard in the trees.

It was all quiet when he passed under the second log. He exited the water and lay down on the warm grass by the rocks. The heat of the rocks dried him quickly, and soon he dozed off.

He had not been asleep long when another sound awoke him. Motionless, he just listened with his eyes closed. Mick had taught him to track animals, which meant using more senses than your eyes. Jack could not smell anything, so whatever it was, it was downwind. It moved very quietly just inside the tree line. Jack knew he would not be able to see it even if he opened his eyes, so he lay motionless and listened. After a minute, the sound was gone. Whatever it was sounded big, although it moved through the trees incredibly quietly. Too quiet for a bear. Jack slowly opened his eyes and looked at the trees where the sound had come from. Nothing was visible as he scanned along the tree line. It was too dark in the dense woods to see inside, so he slowly sat up, listening all the time. Nothing. So, he dressed and put his pack on.

The four-mile run back to the cabin was pleasant. The smooth downhill trail lulled him into a faster pace than he had planned, but it felt great to feel free in the forest again. It always made him feel like a primitive man chasing his meal. He returned to the cabin with hours of daylight left and set his sights on making dinner.

10

After Jack had trained for a week up in the mountains, he knew he had made the right decision to come up there and train. His body was beginning to feel rested and ready for anything, even though he was running at a higher altitude than normal. For the past five days after running to the crater, Jack ran a long, slow twelve to twenty miles along the smooth dirt trails around the mountain. The slow pace allowed his body and mind to recover and acclimate. The trails around the crater felt right, like home, and he often lost track of time.

The last track season had been especially hard. His race times were slower than they should have been. To make up for it, he ran more races. The extra races helped the team's scores. The downside was the extra races had taken a toll on body and mind, even though he had not run his fastest.

Here on the mountain in a week, he was beginning to feel his spirits rise—as if his true self wanted to come out and play. The easy pace and long runs gave him time to think.

He always thought about Michelle. *Is she thinking about me?* He had told Michelle he'd come in every week. He knew he had to pick up more socks and underwear as he packed eight pairs of running shoes but only five pairs of socks and underwear. That meant he had to do laundry more often. In a week, he'd start twice-daily workouts. Two weeks after that, three workouts a day would begin, and so would washing socks daily. He had better ways to spend his free time than washing clothes in the cold, cold water from the river.

Don't kid yourself, he thought. *Yes, clothing is necessary, and her cooking is great, but seeing Michelle is number one.*

* * *

Early the next morning, Jack loaded the five-gallon kerosene can into the back of the truck before leaving. He had stayed up late reading textbooks by kerosene lamp and had used the extra at the cabin. He did not want to use the computer room because it meant talking to Uncle Mick again, and he didn't feel ready for that. Uncle Mick had not put lights in the main room, and Jack wanted to sit by the fire, so he had to use the kerosene lamp.

He always did well in school but found the material easier to read and comprehend at the cabin without outside distractions. He thought about the work required to get his Ph.D. and thought the cabin was the place to stay when he started working on it. That is if he went for it. Four years straight of college was enough for anybody. Jack was not in a hurry, so he would cross that bridge when he came to it.

The four-mile drive to town went by quickly. Jack thought about how much he enjoyed running the trails around the crater instead of the road to town. It was harder, but it made him feel more at peace. He hadn't yet run on the road because he might be tempted to stop in town and see Michelle. If he did that, he knew he wouldn't want to return to the cabin alone and train.

The parking area for the café was full as he approached. Breakfast must be a moneymaker for Michelle, not that she really needed it now.

When Jack walked through the front door, heads turned, and everyone stopped talking. The quiet was deafening. Then they all started talking to him simultaneously, and Jack had to raise his arms to stop them.

Michelle looked up from the plate she was serving and, with a serious look on her face, said, "Hey, Lobo . . . it looks as though you were not just telling a story about being Mick's only living heir."

The others stayed quiet as Jack stood still, considering what he would say.

"OK, I really need to tell you all something first. You are all my family. I feel so blessed to have you as my family." His eyes filled with tears as men and women with tears in their own eyes jumped up and came over to him, patting him, tapping him on the shoulder, or giving him quick hugs.

Finally, when it looked like it would never stop, Michelle hollered, "How about giving him a chance to answer? Can't you see the man needs coffee?" People returned to their seats and went back to their breakfasts.

Jack sat on a stool by the bar surveying the room. Michelle brought Jack coffee and asked, "Can I fix you a plate?"

"Of your fantastic cooking?" he asked. "Heck, yes! You can't imagine how tired I am of my own cooking after just a week," said Jack.

Michelle paused on her way to the kitchen when the questions began.

As usual, Bear was the first to speak. "Jack, what are your plans now that you are the . . . well . . . chief of our tribe?

"What?" said Jack. "Who said anything about me being chief of our tribe?"

"Jack, you may not know this, but over the last thirty years, Mick slowly gathered us here in this town from all over the globe. We had been scattered for our protection, and now with the end date nearing, Mick wanted us back together for strength," Bear said.

"That and we all had to help. He could not trust outsiders to do the job. While we were away, we all went to school to learn specific skills. Living a long time means you have a long time to study, which was needed for the slow ones," he said, laughing heartily, as the rest of the room joined in.

"We all talked after you left and saw the news report that night. Mick was our shaman and chief. We all want you to be our shaman and chief as well. But don't worry because we are all here to teach and help, seeing you are still inexperienced."

Jack looked from one to the other as they smiled at him. *My family . . . they all really are my family*, he thought. Then, it suddenly dawned on him that Michelle must be a tribal member herself. He looked over at her and, with a worried expression on his face, asked, "Uh, Michelle, you're not my cousin or something, are you?" Michelle and the rest of the people in the cafe burst out laughing.

Michelle walked over to Jack and pulled him into a hug, "No, Jack, I am not your cousin. I am a member of the tribe, but we are not related. I did not know I was Native, let alone a member of this tribe, until Mick figured it out. Mick said it was weird I would choose this place of all places to come. He did a background check and a bit of blood work, which determined my parents were indeed members of the tribe. My father had died in a work accident and my mother died in childbirth. I never knew who they were until Mick found out the whole story about three years ago."

"But your eyes are green!" Jack said.

"Yes, my green eyes fooled everyone, including me. Mick told me to keep it quiet until things were ready." With that, she leaned over and gave Jack a quick kiss on the cheek.

Jack's face grew red, and he grinned and looked down. He was sure he was as red as a tomato. As laughter once again filled the room, Jack quickly grabbed his coffee and buried his face in the cup.

Bear once again spoke. "Jack, we really would like you to be our chief as well as our shaman. Mick told us about our first shaman who was white-haired and blue-eyed.

"Now that we know your story, we understand your importance to our tribe and why Mick kept you separate from us. It was in the event if anything happened to him, you would be there for us. Jack, we understand what we are asking. There's no hurry. You have time to catch up on our history."

Jack was silent, seemingly deep in thought. Then he said, "Yes, Bear, I will be your chief and shaman if each one of you teaches me what you know."

A dozen voices rose, all assenting, then a single voice said, "Bear teaching everything he knows should only take three or four minutes." Again, everyone burst out in laughter at Bear's expense. But Bear was laughing too and sat back down.

"Now, can we take a break?" Jack asked. "Michelle's promised to make me one of her delicious breakfasts. With that, she dashed into the kitchen, returning in short order with a steaming plate of food.

Conversation rose in the room as a schedule was made for each to get together with Jack to tell him what they knew of the past and what Mick had told them so Jack could see the whole picture. Each of them knew they had important information the others did not know. Mick made sure no one person knew too much, so if they were caught or lost, what they knew would not affect the tribe too greatly. After arrangements were made, the people began to disperse.

Bear came over to Jack's table. "Lobo, you are now the center of our tribe. Until last week you were our friend. Now we know you are our family. Every tribal member always felt there was something special about you, but only Mick really knew what it was. I hope you learn what it is and tell us. Our lives and future are in your hands." Bear patted Jack on the back and walked out into the sunshine.

Michelle, the only one left, smiled at Jack. "So, my Lobo, you are more than just the cute boy I was friends with so many years ago. I have watched you grow and saw how Mick took such a special interest in you. In the beginning, I thought it was because you were such a great runner. Now I know he saw you as our future. It looks as though you've quite the job ahead of you, my Jack.

"With just a little over twenty years before the treaty is up, crucial details must be negotiated. Don't look so worried, you won't have to do all that. Mick has been training people for years for that task. Your job is to finish school, run like the Lobo you are, and lead us into our future.

"Mick told me years ago our true leader would be here soon. I had no idea it would be you. I also know you need to finish what you started. Mick wanted school and running to be your focus." She got a faraway look in her eyes and said, "I know you must run now to lead us in the future. Don't ask me how I know that because I am unsure."

Jack looked at Michelle. At that moment, it was as if he knew they were meant for one another—for now and for eternity. But did she feel the same? *Maybe she just wants to be good friends with me. But our connection seems deeper than that.*

Michelle broke the mood as she looked around at the dirty dishes and said, "OK, mister, let's clean up and talk while we do. I am sure we both have questions. I need to prep before the lunch crowd. You had better get out of here right after we clean up."

"I know I should, but I want to stay for a while."

"Lobo, I want nothing more than that, but there are three things keeping you from staying. One, you must keep training. Two, someone may come here looking for a story because they might have figured out that this was Mick's café and he had lived here sometimes. And three, I can only hold back Bear and the rest just so long before they tease you mercilessly about being my boyfriend."

"OK, the last reason is good enough," Jack laughed. "I'll help you clean up before I head out."

As they both began bussing the tables and stacking the dirty dishes in the kitchen, Michelle said, "Jack, did you know Mick put a computer in the office down here at the café? He told me he put one up at the cabin as well. I don't use my computer often," she said, "but we can email, and video chat."

"Of course."

"Why don't we check in with each other every night before bed if we want to."

"Want to?" said Jack. "How about we will?"

When they had cleaned the last of the pans, Jack said, "I guess I'd better head out."

"Wait a minute, I've got a care package for you."

"What kind of care package?"

"Oh, just some home cooking."

Jack let out a yell, picked her up, and spun her around. "You are the best, Michelle."

"So, is it me or my food you like more?"

Jack smiled and said, "Let me think." That reply earned him a quick snap from a towel.

After they put the food into the truck, Jack said, "Oh wait, I just remembered I need to buy more socks and underwear."

Michelle let out a hoot and then said, "Food and hugs, I can understand, but socks and underwear?"

"Well, I need more. I'll have to head over to Randle and buy them. And I need some kerosene too."

"Probably not a good idea with all the news about you, Jack," said Michelle. "Anyway, I haven't thrown any of Mick's things away, and you two probably wear the same size. I think Mick would be happy to save you money. Not that you need to worry about money," she said with a smile.

"You know Mick as well as I do. He wouldn't approve of me spending money I don't need to."

Jack opened the door to Mick's bedroom, which was a mess. Mick had never married and wasn't especially tidy. He remembered the first time he had been to Mick's after Michelle arrived, nine years before. He walked into the house and stopped. At first, he thought he had walked into the wrong house because it was so clean. Before Jack could say anything, Michelle came out of the kitchen but stopped when she saw Jack.

He was only twelve, but at already five-feet-nine inches tall and lean, he looked taller. His shoulder-length white hair and blue eyes set him apart in any crowd. Michelle, who was about five-feet-ten inches tall and could look slightly down at him, smiled and said, "Who are you, young man?"

Jack hadn't been able to utter a word. Mick came to Jack's rescue and introduced them. Michelle interrupted his thoughts by pointing out the top two drawers of the bureau. When he opened the top drawer, he found socks, including a dozen pair of new running socks in Jack's size. It was obvious Mick had bought them so Jack would not run out while visiting.

The second drawer held new packages of underwear; Jack was surprised to find at least a dozen pairs of running shorts. Besides, Jack found the usual t-shirts, socks, underwear, and running tights still in packages.

"Take whatever you can use," Michelle urged. Jack knew that was exactly what Mick would have wanted and picked out what he thought he would need most. He knew he could return for other things if he needed them.

Jack stopped for kerosene at the gas station. He knew Michelle was right. He had to go back to the cabin for his safety, and he had to train, or he would never achieve his goals. The drive back to the cabin seemed to take twice as long as the trip into town. But now he'd be able to email Michelle, which would make staying up at the cabin much easier. Jack smiled and began planning his workouts for the next few weeks.

At the cabin, he unloaded his supplies and the food, then got ready for a run. He had missed a couple runs but had gotten a full day's rest. With rest and the good food in him, Jack decided he would run fast the hard six-mile loop in the crater. He had been doing easier long runs lately, but he was ready for the test.

11

A s always, the four-mile run up to the crater was the perfect warm-up. The slow pace allowed him to warm up his muscles, and the scenery made the distance fly by. By the time Jack arrived at the crater, the sun was just peeking over the rim, but the temperature was still cool and comfortable for a hard run. The early summer nights meant the rocks would be cool, and the weather was not too warm for a hard run.

Jack finished his warmup stretches and sprints on the flats by the lake and prepared to run. It had been over two years since he had run the crater, and he was itching to get going. His love for running was born in this crater. Uncle Mick had run with him at first, but after age twelve, Jack usually ran alone. There just seemed to be a drive coming from inside that pushed him harder than any coach could have. Mick had been fast, but he ran for the love of running, whereas Jack was obsessed with winning.

After Jack was granted his guardian, he determined he wanted to beat it. Mick said no runner in the history of the tribe had ever beaten his guardian. Now, Jack understood just what that really meant. No shaman had ever beaten his guardian. Uncle Mick must have been the only runner in this crater for the last 300 years. If the tribe first came here 20,000 years ago, and each shaman lived 300 years, then there had only been over sixty shaman running in this crater. Jack had always thought Mick built the running trails around the crater. No, those smooth trails had been made by sixty men, each running for 300 years.

Why had so many men run here for so many centuries? Was the reason the love of running, or was there something else? Was it their way of becoming one with nature? Putting those questions aside, Jack thought, *Now it's my turn.*

Even though the crater was at 4,000 feet, Jack ran with ease. The first mile was flat and always an easy warm-up and not too bad for training. Now he had only five more miles to go.

As he started uphill for the second mile, the excitement of running started to flow through Jack as it had not for the past two years. The second mile was a wonderful test of endurance, and Jack realized how much he had missed this place as his heart rate climbed as quickly as the altitude.

As he ascended the trail up the crater, he heard a noise. *Ah, there it is. My guardian is here.* Even after all these years, he was surprised when he heard the running just inside the woods. But there was a comfort in knowing there was something up here with him as he ran. In the city, there was no one who could match him step for step.

Up here, Jack always knew he had a ready opponent. Of course, he had never beaten the guardian, but there was still time. He might live as long as Uncle Mick. The thought of living 200 or 300 years was going through his mind as he reached the two-mile point and the top of the first climb.

Just before starting the third mile, he looked around as always. He was still almost a thousand feet from the rim of the crater, but he could now see Mt. Rainier. As Jack started the third mile, the first mile downhill, he realized he was not even winded.

With a smile, Jack ran smoothly back down toward the crater floor. The sound of his tireless guardian, who was running no more than forty feet to his side in the thick trees above him, comforted him.

He reached the bottom of the downhill section and the end of the third mile. *Yes, I've still got it.*

Just then, something up the crater caught his eye. A closer look showed there had been a huge rockslide at least fifty feet across. It had not been there two years ago. But suddenly, he felt something was not right. Jack moved closer to take a look.

The slide had gone down the face and across the trail, but the trail looked perfect. He knew the trail should have been damaged because there was damage on both sides of the trail. Who had restored the trail? And where did those trees come from? Trees had been planted that were twenty to thirty feet tall. Whoever had planted them had to be strong or used a helicopter.

It was then he noticed the silence. He could no longer hear his guardian. The sounds of the guardian in the forest had stopped just before he reached the slide clearing. The new trees that had been planted were not thick enough to hide the guardian, so it had stopped and advanced no further.

What is it anyway? Jack was about to go back up hill for the fourth mile when he again heard his guardian. *Someday, I am going to catch a glimpse of the guardian . . . someday.*

The fourth mile was always the hardest, and today was no exception. Halfway up, he began to tire. Two years of running at sea level and the altitude was getting to him. One week had not been enough to acclimate him. *Gut it out, and you have gravy downhill*, he told himself, *that is if you don't die first.* Jack pushed all the harder.

As he reached the top of the climb, he knew he had to reduce the pace down the other side. Tired as he was, the beauty of this place made all the pain worthwhile. Yes, he could run here for 300 years if given the chance. Jack promised himself that he'd have enough time to not only see his guardian but beat it as well.

At the bottom of the hill, he felt better during the fifth mile, even though it was downhill. One more mile to go and he was done, and that one was flat. Without a second thought, Jack decided to go for it and sped up. He was running fast, but sure enough, his guardian had caught up and was right there, hidden by the forest. The guardian always seemed to run easily, but this summer would be the year he would beat it.

The trees flew by. A breeze off the lake cooled Jack just a bit, and he gave it a little more. He could see the finish log and pushed a bit harder. He crossed the line and slowed to a stop breathing heavily, pleased even though he knew it was not his fastest run. Not too bad for the first time in over two years, especially the last mile.

After a cool drink of water, he plunged into the lake. While he swam, he thought about people who didn't run. They wouldn't be able to understand why someone would want to train to run so fast it hurt. Or be excited about the thought of running for 300 years. What they didn't know about running fast is it didn't hurt. The desire to win overrode all else.

Mick used to tell him, "Jack, you were born to race." He was right. He had always wanted to win . . . in running anyway. He did not mind winning at other sports, but losing at them didn't rip his soul apart like losing at running did. Although it had been years since he had lost, except to his guardian.

I'm going to beat my guardian before I go back to school in the fall, he silently vowed.

After a refreshing swim and a snack, Jack ignored the desire to take a nap in the warm sun. A nap could wait until he got back to the cabin. He had a question for Mick's computer and did not want to wait to ask it.

12

During his run back to the cabin, Jack wondered who had fixed the trail and planted the trees. Maybe Mick had planned for this in the event of his death and had a crew come up to take care of things after his death. But Mick had said no person other than a shaman could go to the crater. He hoped he could find the answers on Mick's computer about the trail and the trees and another question he had on his mind. Arriving at the cabin, Jack dropped his gear and went right into the new computer room. He placed his hand on the palm reader and the room came alive once again. Jack thought hard and then said, "Uncle Mick, I have a question."

Mick's face popped up in an instant. "Nice to see you again, Lobo. What is your question today?"

"Hi Mick," said Jack, not sure if the computer could understand the greeting, but he liked saying it. It made the whole thing seem somehow more real.

"Mick, I was running at the crater and noticed there had been a rockslide. Also noticed someone had repaired the trail. Can you tell me who fixed it?"

Mick's face remained frozen for a moment, and then he spoke. "Lobo, there are questions that cannot be answered currently. You have important things to learn before that question can be answered. Forgive me for what seems like a secret, but it is necessary that you learn things for yourself. You might say this is one of the tests you will encounter. You must gain knowledge for the answers you seek. May I help you in any other way?"

Jack sat quietly, thinking as Mick's image froze.

"Uncle Mick, I have a question. Is Michelle meant for me?"

It took only a second before Mick started laughing. He laughed for at least ten seconds before settling down. "Sorry about that, Lobo. That was one of the questions Jim thought of early on, and he caught me off guard with it then. That is the kind of question all men face, and I am unable to answer. I can say she is a fine person. Her spirit is strong. You might say she wrapped me around her finger hundreds of times. I would be fearful of crossing her. Rarely was the time, my boy, I did not do what she told me to do."

Again, Mick laughed hard, and this time for quite a while. When he stopped laughing, he became serious. "Lobo, if you find Michelle to be the love you choose, you can do no better. Be forewarned, though, for she is as wild as any spirit can be, but she will never fail you."

Jack looked at the screen silently and then said, "Thank you, Mick. I will see you soon." The screen went blank.

As he walked out into the main room, he was in deep thought. The feelings he had for Michelle felt like love, but he had never had a girlfriend before. He wished he had someone close by that he could ask questions about relationships. This would have to be between Michelle and him—they would have to work it out.

Still thinking about how to talk to Michelle about their relationship, he ran into the table. He did not have his shoes on and kicked the table hard. "Oww," he said as he hopped around the room, saying a few choice words.

Right then, he heard Michelle's voice ask, "Are you OK, Lobo?"

What? Jack looked around and asked, "Are you here, Michelle? Is that you?" He did not get an answer and sat down in one of the overstuffed chairs. *That was weird! Man, I must be losing it, I could have sworn I heard Michelle.*

He figured he was just tired from the run and needed to eat, or maybe he should have taken a nap. When he checked his foot, it was sore but not really hurt. He stood up to go grab something to eat and email Michelle.

Maybe I feel guilty for doubting my feelings for her, and that made me think I heard her voice.

* * *

The next day, Jack woke early as usual and ate a light breakfast before his morning run. Checking his email, he had an answer from Michelle to his light-hearted email last night. He had thanked her again for all the wonderful food she had sent with him. He was surprised at how good getting an email from her made him feel. She had laughed at his teasing and was glad he appreciated the food. She said she would send food back with him every week when he came to town.

But a chill ran down his spine when he read the next line. "How's your foot, Jack?" she had written.

How could she know about my foot? After emailing Michelle back, Jack closed the computer and went outside.

He still had goose bumps. He didn't know what to think about all this weird stuff. Two weeks ago, he was just an ordinary kid in college. Now he was filthy rich, and they were telling him he was a shaman, a chief, and was going to live for 300 years. What's more, the girl he had always loved seemed to be able to read his mind, and he could talk to a dead man via a computer! All he wanted to do was run, and now he was buried up to his armpits in strange happenings.

He had studied science and wanted to be a scientist after graduation, so he thought, *I should be able to figure this out.*It was time to put on his running gear and go for a mind-clearing run. Forget about all that crazy stuff.

Today he'd run toward the crater on the river trail. The trail was smooth and easy to run on, and the river made a nice distraction even when he was running at a slower pace.

About a mile away from the cabin, Jack heard something. Whatever it was, it was keeping pace with him just inside the deep brush. He kept running and listening, wondering, *What could this be so far from the crater?* He knew a bear could not run that quietly, so what was it? *Maybe it's my guardian!* But that could not be because he had never heard it outside the crater.

He wasn't really afraid, just mostly curious as he turned into the forest toward the noise. In about twenty feet, he found a spot where he could easily get through the underbrush. He had to slow to a walk and push his way through. After about thirty feet, the thick brush thinned out. As the foliage thinned, he could see farther. The thick canopy of the forest kept the underbrush from growing thick like it was near the edges where the sun was. The trees inside were giant old-growth trees. Once his eyes got accustomed to the dimmer light, he could see quite a distance.

He could have driven a truck between the trees without hitting a single bush or tree.

The sound he had been hearing stopped once he entered the underbrush. Now, inside the trees, it was silent. He walked further into the forest, searching for what was making the elusive sound.

Walking slowly, Jack noticed his footsteps did not make a sound on the moss-covered forest floor. If his footsteps didn't make a sound here, what kind of animal could have? It would be impossible for a deer or a bear to make a sound on this soft surface. He walked for a while longer but didn't see anything that could have made those sounds. Finding no trace of an animal, he made his way back to the river trail to finish the run.

Jack knew he would come back and search again for what made those sounds. It was a plus finding that old-growth forest because it would be a perfect place to run in the future. The forest floor was soft, totally clear of brush, and would make a great training place.

But there was the matter of the creature making the sounds. He hadn't heard anything more since he first entered the thick brush into the forest floor. Whatever had made the sounds must have run away. If he heard it again, he would just have to try harder to find it. Given enough time, he thought he could figure out what it was.

If it was his guardian, why did it come down here? No way he would dare ask Mick until he knew more.

* * *

Over the next few days, he heard the sounds on every run, and his curiosity was running high. No matter how fast he ran toward it when he heard it, he was never able to catch a glimpse of who or what was making it. Whatever or whoever, it was really fast.

He would have bet any amount of money it was his guardian. *Come to think about it, I now have the money to bet,* Jack thought, and he grinned.

One day, five days since he had run the crater hard, he was again ready to give the crater a go. The weather was perfect that morning. After breakfast, he headed up to take on his guardian and see how it could run that day. He wanted to beat the heat of the sun.

Today might be the day I kick my guardian's butt, thought Jack. Nothing felt better to him than when his legs were rested before a tough run. He thought about how Mick and the elders really had made a good decision to build the cabin where it was. The four miles to the crater were a perfect warm-up for the six-mile hard run, and the run back was the perfect cool-down.

As usual, the scenery running to the crater made Jack's heart soar. It was hard to imagine his people had run this same trail for 20,000 years. It was hard to imagine a finer place in the world to run.

It's true, Native Americans should not ever live in a city.

In those two years locked away at the college, Jack had lost himself. He vowed never again to stay away from the mountain cabin and trails for so long. Even when he got back to school, he could come up on weekends to train if there were no conflicts.

Man, I'm feeling great.

He had been doing three workouts most days for the past two weeks and was feeling like his old self.

He was glad he had brought so many pairs of running shoes as he was afraid the terrain and number of miles he ran would wear out a couple pair in two or three weeks. Fast speedwork requires light shoes for the fastest times and top speeds. Jack had brought two pairs of light training flats but today was the first day he would use them. With three months left to train, he would not wear them often for fear of completely wearing them out. But today, they felt soft on the feet, so light they made him feel he could almost fly.

Today Jack felt especially good physically and mentally with not an ounce of fatigue.

Hope they do make me fly today, he thought. His leg muscles felt so loose as if he did not even need to stretch.

He was so deep in thought mile one flew by in an instant and at a fast pace, according to his watch. He had almost forgotten to check the watch, and when he looked, the time was a pleasant surprise. Memories of his first time running here with Mick flowed through his head when he hit that mark. With a deep sigh, Jack imagined how wonderful it would be to run with Uncle Mick once more.

The first mile felt easy, although it was fast, but now came the first hill. He had run about a hundred feet up the hill when he heard the guardian running parallel to him in the trees. Smiling, he kept running up the steep hill. At the top, he was pleasantly surprised to see he had run the second mile faster than his last workout here. It looked like he was getting fitter each week. The downhill third mile was always easy, and the time at the bottom was faster than the last time. This run turned out to be the fastest and easiest so far.

As Jack reached the rockslide, the guardian stopped inside the tree line, out of sight like last time. He could use that information to beat the guardian as his speed improved. He could daydream only for a minute because the second uphill mile loomed ahead. Last time he had sucked wind halfway up the hill and felt heavy. Today, he was feeling good, and his times were fast. When he reached the top of the hill and saw his time, he was elated. Jack had run the second uphill mile faster than ever and still felt great.

As he flew downhill on the fifth mile, the sounds of the guardian's smooth strides eating up the terrain easily made him smile. For just a second, he feared he would never beat his guardian, but he quickly buried that thought and accelerated down the hill. Jack's time at the bottom of the hill was also faster than any other time before, and he felt he could run faster yet. The way he felt with a mile to go, it was easy to really let loose and see what he had left. He felt this could easily be his fastest mile ever run in the crater and went for it.

The lightness in his legs allowed him to run faster and faster as he flew around the lake. Running on the flats was easy compared to hills, and he took advantage of feeling so good. With about a half mile to go, he pressed even harder. He was rewarded at the finish with his fastest time ever run here.

Amazingly, he still felt good at the end of the run. After a cool-down jog, Jack decided he had earned a swim and a nap. After his swim, he lay in the warm, soft grass for a much-deserved snooze.

He remembered to set the watch alarm for two hours. Jack had to get back to the cabin, eat, do chores, and go for an evening run, so he did not want to oversleep. He dreamt of running the crater trail while Mick, his mom and dad, and his sister yelled encouragement. Somehow, they kept up with him no matter how fast he ran.

With a start, he woke and sat up. Jack had not thought about his family often over the past two years, and that dream really shook him. Getting up, he started walking around the lake, the dream vivid in his mind.

He thought about the family he had lost. While they were alive, he never knew they were his true birth family. Being adopted had been OK with Jack because it meant they had chosen him because they loved him. Now that he knew they were his real family, the pain of missing them had deepened. He knew his dad, mom, and Mick had told him he was adopted to keep him safe. As it turned out, they were right. He could have very well been killed when they were if it was known he was Mick's heir. They each gave up an incredible amount of themselves to ensure he was safe.

If only I could see them all one more time. The next time he was lucky enough to dream of them, he wouldn't try to wake himself.

Time to head back. Chores didn't do themselves, and there was a four-mile run ahead before he was home, as well as an evening run to go. On the easy run down to the cabin, Jack thought about his wonderful childhood. His parents were the best parents a kid could hope for, and they sacrificed an amazing amount to keep him safe. His kid sister was always a kick to have around, and they never had any problems getting along. He knew there was no way to turn back the clock and see them again, but he could honor their lives by being the best he could be.

He reached the cabin in great spirits. After eating and doing the chores, he was off to do an easy six-mile evening run. Tomorrow would be Sunday, and time to head back to town. Email was nice, but Jack was eager to see Michelle. She was his best friend, had a great smile, and made the most delicious food. He'd better remember to keep that order straight, or she'd have his hide.

13

J ack was up just before dawn the next morning to get in a run before heading into town. In case he had to stay late, he didn't want to lose an entire day of training, no matter how tasty Michelle's food was. He also needed to burn the extra calories or gain weight from her cooking.

It was still too dark outside to run, so he had time to check his email. Sure enough, Michelle had sent him an email.

What he read set his heart pounding. Michelle wrote that there were about half a dozen strangers hanging around the place asking questions. She said Sheriff Donald stopped them for minor traffic offenses and ran their driver's licenses. What he discovered confirmed his worst suspicions—they were journalists from news agencies. The sheriff's guess was they somehow figured out Mick spent time here and were trying to find out if Jack was somewhere around town.

"Our tribe is friendly to strangers, but we don't give away information easily," Michelle wrote. "In fact, no one outside our tribe knows Mick owned the restaurant or the house, and the cabin is off everyone's radar. Bear and a couple of the guys camouflaged the entrance to the road to your cabin days ago. They made it look like the road had been closed for years."

For now, the cabin was safe, but he was trapped.

Jack sat and thought and then got an idea. He sent an email to Jim, who answered right away. Jim told him what was happening with the reporters and that the press was hanging around at the places thought to be Mick's hangouts. They smelled a story and were not going to let it go. They were like sharks to blood. Then Jack proposed an idea to Jim of how to draw them away.

Jack told Jim to leave his office out the back door as if he were trying to get away secretly, but not to be too good about it. They expected the press to follow him no matter where he went.

"Jim, do you have access to an airplane?"

Jim wrote back, "Sure. Mick owns five or six small airlines."

"Great," said Jack. "Now, go to the airport and file a flight plan to somewhere in India. Make sure anyone near you hears you make the call, especially about a flight to India.

Jim typed, "Brilliant, but I'm not really looking forward to taking such a long flight."

"No problem," came Jack's reply. "Call ahead. Since we own the airline, we can do what we want. You will fly first class, and first class is always boarded first. Once on the plane, you climb down the hatch into the cargo area, lay on a baggage carrier, and have the baggage handlers cover you. Once completely covered, have them take you into the baggage shipping area in the terminal. From there, have one of our private cars pick you up. Keep up the hide-and-seek until they get tired of chasing shadows. Anyway, Jim, isn't it about time you really took a vacation?"

Jim's reply came quickly. "Well, with everything happening, I have not had a real one in years."

"Then it's settled. Why don't you plan to take four weeks of vacation starting now and go wherever you would like to go—like how about a quiet beach somewhere?"

"Guess I have to listen to my boss," messaged Jim.

Jack laughed and signed off.

With the diversion plan in the works, it was time to see how well it would unfold. Jack grabbed the gear needed for the morning, jumped into the truck, and drove toward town. He parked the truck out of sight about half a mile from the main roadway and began jogging. Sure enough, the guys had blocked the entrance to the road with piles of rocks and logs. It looked as though no one had driven up that road for years. *Leave it to a Native American to be able to cover tracks so well,* thought Jack, feeling proud to be the tribe's chief.

He advanced cautiously toward town on a well-worn trail about 400 feet from the road, the same trail the kids rode their dirt bikes around town without getting in trouble for riding on the road.

When he made his way to Michelle's back door and went inside. It was already 10:00 a.m., and she was at the café getting ready for Sunday brunch. So, he went out the back door and crept his way to the back door of the café. As he walked through the kitchen, he kept low in case anyone was looking through the window. He could hear Michelle, Bear and a couple of others talking out front. With one look over the counter, it was obvious the coast was clear, and he stepped out. He was met with a chorus of "Hey Jack, good to see you!"

"What are you doing here?" asked Michelle. "I was worried about you."

Jack told them the plan he had set up with Jim, and they all got a kick out of that.

"Well, it worked," said Bear. "Half an hour ago, those vultures got in their cars and headed out of here like a pack of wolves on the hunt. Jack, seriously, that was a nice deception. Smart work! That was worthy of a real war chief."

Bear's remark filled Jack with warmth and pride.

"Are you hungry?" asked Michelle. "You've earned a special meal for sure."

Before he could answer, she was off to the kitchen. "Don't forget something for your other hungry customers as well," said Bear followed by his booming laugh.

"Bear, you and the guys did great," said Jack, sitting down. "You covered the cabin road perfectly."

"Lobo, we figured the reporters would be too busy in town and too lazy to walk up that road even if they thought there might be something worth looking at."

"Looks like your plan will keep them away for a while."

Jack told them Jim would surface in Hawaii in two or three days and give a press announcement. From there, he would pick his following destinations. Then after resting for a day or two, Jim would call another press conference before taking off again.

"We are going to send them all over the globe over the next few weeks, or longer, depending on the amount of vacation Jim wants. He said he could use a holiday, but he is also planning on meeting with our company holdings around the world. All he needs to do is stay a day or two ahead of the press and then surface with another press briefing." Michelle came out of the kitchen, balancing an armload of plates and returned to the kitchen for more. When she was done, she sat down with them and said, "Eat up, boys." Everyone just stared at their plates. They had been eating Michelle's food for years, but she had outdone herself this time.

Bear looked at Jack and said, "Lobo, you need to come to town more often." Everyone laughed, and they all dug in.

After eating, everyone seemed relieved that the situation was resolved, but no one wanted to talk.

Finally, Jack said, "Bear, I need you to get everyone together in small groups and let them know what we are going to do," instructed Jack. "We don't want to make anyone outside our tribe suspicious, but we need to make plans to protect ourselves from them coming in and bothering us.

"First, everyone must keep on doing whatever it is they normally do. Second, you need to decide on a signal so we all know if strangers are in town. No phones or emails. Use a visible sign, like a porchlight or a flag. It will be up to you to decide what you use, but let me know what it is so I don't mess up.

"I'll stay connected with Michelle while at the cabin. Mick was wise enough to put a secure computer line at the cabin and one in Michelle's house. If you need to get any information to me, go through her. Now everyone should go about their business and enjoy the quiet, at least, for now."

When they were gone, Michelle said, "Want to help me clean up?"

"What? Me cleanup?" he said. "I am the rich boss, remember? You don't expect me to clean up, do you?"

"Here's the way it works," said Michelle with a grin. "You will clean up or not eat, Chief."

While they were washing dishes, Jack asked about her email comment about his foot.

"Oh, yes, your foot," she said. "I was wondering how it felt after you ran into the table."

"Michelle, I was at my cabin when I ran into the table. There is no way you could have known about it."

"No, you are wrong, Jack. You did it here. I remember. I was lying on the sofa taking a nap, and you ran into the table."

"Michelle, I was at my cabin barefoot and hit the table. When I yelled out in pain, I heard you ask if I was OK."

"Are you sure, Jack?"

"Yes, I'm sure!"

Michelle did not look up for a while after that. She kept staring into the sink. After a short silence, she asked, "Jack, is there something weird about us? Have you noticed things are strange when we are together?"

"Yes," Jack said, "but strange in a good way." Jack reached out for her hand and looked into her eyes. "Michelle, I don't know if all couples have this connection or if it is just us. But it makes our relationship special. I feel connected with you in a way I didn't know was possible, and it feels wonderful. I want to be more than friends. It feels like we are meant to be together. We can keep each other safe if need be." He stopped talking momentarily and then asked, "Michelle, are you alright with all the weirdness?"

"Oh, I am, my silly Lobo."

Then to cut the solemn moment, Jack dipped his hand in the soapy sink and flicked Michelle with the suds. A splash fight broke out, with them laughing and chasing each other through the kitchen.

Later, when they were sitting on the sofa at Michelle's house, she turned to him with a serious look on her expressive face and said, "Jack," she said, "I wonder what it would be like to spend the rest of our lives together."

"What a wonderfully long life that would be. . . ." he said smiling.

"What do you mean?"

"You don't know?"

"Know what?

Jack sighed. "Oh, do I have something big to tell you." He then told her what Mick had told him about his longevity as she listened quietly.

Michelle was stunned. "You can't be serious!"

"Yes, Michelle, I am."

"I never knew . . . or suspected. Mick never told me all the years I was living and working here."

"Michelle, he probably didn't tell you because he didn't want to reveal too much too soon."

"Maybe he didn't want to scare me off, knowing I might have to live around Mister Lobo Running Man forever," she said.

The afternoon passed as they relaxed, talked, and enjoyed spending time together. Finally, Michelle got up and said, "I'm going to make us something to eat. Are you going for your evening run while I make dinner?"

Jack knew the trails behind the house were covered with soft moss and were a dream to run on. As he put his running shoes on, he thought of all the times he had run these trails barefoot as a young kid. He could have run barefoot that afternoon and enjoyed every soft step on the moss. But Mick always said he might cut his feet on a broken branch or sharp rock, and if that happened, he would miss days of training. So he insisted Jack wore running shoes when he ran to prevent injuries. Two exceptions were when running in sand or soft grass.

When he got back to Michelle's house, it smelled like he thought heaven should smell. They were quiet that night while they ate. Then

Michelle looked at Jack and asked, "Do you think you will get tired of me if we live for hundreds of years?"

He looked at her and said honestly, "I could never get tired of you."

Michelle reached for Jack's hand, looked into his pale-blue eyes, and said, "The Great Spirit has destined us to be together."

It was late when Michelle walked him up the trail to the truck. Together they carried the food she had made for him. They hugged by the truck in silence for quite a while. Jack hated to leave the one he had waited for his entire life, even if she'd only be four miles away.

"Email everyday as always," she said.

"Yes, every day. Also, I can keep you posted as to what Jim is doing and where he is leading the press off to, if you want."

She gave a snort and broke out laughing. "Oh, Lobo, just the thought of the press running all over the world chasing you makes me laugh. Imagine how crazy they will be when you return to college and run races."

As Jack got into the truck and drove off toward the cabin, he thought about what living for so many years might be like. Shaking his head, he thought, *Can't think about that now. It's crazy!*

14

At the start of Jack's third week at the cabin, he felt like he could live there forever. There was something about this place that felt right. Jack understood why Mick stayed close. This mountain had been home to their tribe for the last 20,000 years. It was in their blood to live near this mountain.

Jack had slowly healed, mentally and physically, on the mountain over the past three weeks. He felt as if his life was finally coming together after losing his parents and Mick.

That morning he felt he needed to do a long recovery run and thought he'd try running the old-growth forest area. With luck, he could find some good training areas before the warm weather hit. The thought of running on the soft forest floor he found when following that strange animal noise intrigued Jack.

Within minutes, he was slowly running up the river trail looking for a thin spot in the brush to go through so he could run the soft forest floor among the huge old-growth trees. Years of Mick's training as a tracker paid off when Jack saw an almost invisible game trail and turned onto it. He carefully picked his way through the thick brush to avoid the sharp branches. The brush was thick for the first twenty feet of the trail. Then, it quickly cleared away, and he could move easily between the spaces between trees.

Jack stopped for five minutes, did some stretching, and let his eyes become accustomed to the dimmer light under the giant western hemlock, western red cedar, and Douglas fir trees. When he was satisfied that he was completely warmed up, he started running at an easy pace. As he ran, he wondered why he had never run in these trees before, especially on hot days when he had to do long runs under the open sun. This day he felt comfortably cool under the trees, and he knew that training on a hot day under these trees would be heaven.

As Jack increased his pace, he realized he was hardly making a sound. The ground under the trees was a mixture of needles, moss, ferns, and composting plant material, all of which made it the softest surface Jack had ever run on. It was too soft to be fast, but a runner would never get sore feet from running on it.

He kept to the edge of the forest and ran parallel to the river to his right so he could hear it flowing over rocks. After about twenty minutes, he encountered a huge fallen giant of a tree and ran along it for 100 feet before he reached a spot near the top of the tree where it was small enough for him to hurdle it.

The moment Jack reached the other side of the tree, he was startled and jumped when he heard the sound of something large running away from him to his left. Jack's sudden hurdle over the tree must have frightened an animal, and it was making a racket trying to get away from him.

It took Jack a second to compose himself and begin searching for the animal. From the loud scratching noises coming from the thick branches to his right, Jack could tell the animal was trying to get over the fallen tree to the side Jack had just come from. He thought he might get a glimpse of whatever it was if he jumped back over the tree. He returned to the top of the downed tree and quickly leaped over to the opposite side.

When his feet silently hit the forest floor on the other side of the tree, he could hear the noise of the animal frantically scrambling to get out of the branches.

Moving away from the fallen tree, he peered through the branches hoping to glimpse what was making so much noise.

About fifty feet away from him, he saw flashes of something that had become entangled in the thick branches of the huge fallen tree. As it broke free of the branches, Jack froze in his tracks.

Suddenly, a large animal with tawny and white skin and black stripes jumped out and turned to face him. Panic filled his mind when he saw the blade-like canine teeth of the animal that was four or five times bigger than a lion—a foot taller than a horse—and very muscular.

What could it be? It was a giant! Then Jack recalled prehistoric renderings he had seen, and then he knew. He was standing just fifty feet from a sabertoothed tiger!

As Jack's muscles tensed and adrenaline flooded his system, he wondered, *How am I going to get away from this huge cat alive?*

But before Jack could sprint away, the tiger suddenly turned and started running away.

Confused, his heart pounding, Jack wondered, *why is he running from me?*

He watched as the tiger began to stumble. Within a dozen strides, the huge cat was staggering as if it were drugged or drunk. In moments, the huge beast was barely crawling. Jack stared at the huge animal in distress, and his panic subsided as he wondered what was wrong with it.

Taking a chance, Jack began slowly walking toward the struggling animal. As he got closer, he could tell the tiger was quickly getting worse and worse. The closer he got, the more the cat struggled. By the time Jack was within twenty feet of it, the cat was barely breathing. Wary, Jack did not want to get closer and began walking in a wide circle around the struggling cat. The suffering animal was impossibly huge. In a section on prehistoric animals in high school, they studied sabertoothed tigers, and he knew this one was larger than normal. There was no way this animal should be alive! He knew they had been extinct for around 12,000 years. The fact that the cat was so huge was what Jack found most difficult to believe.

As he walked around the cat, he kept about twenty feet between them. He noticed it breathing easier and struggling a bit less. Standing opposite the giant cat, he watched it begin to regain its strength. What would happen if it got well enough to get up and attack him? Jack thought it best not to find out but to jump back over the tree, head back to the cabin, and call for help.

As soon as he moved closer to the monster cat to jump to the other side of the tree, the cat began struggling, and its breathing worsened. Jack had run about thirty-five feet past the tiger when he stopped and turned to look back at the cat lying on the ground. He realized he had been upwind of the huge cat when it fell. This might have been the first time he had been upwind of it. When he was downwind, the cat seemed to get better, and now that he was upwind again, it was getting weaker. As he began walking back toward the huge cat, it increasingly struggled to breathe with every step he took closer. As he carefully approached the cat, Jack could see how scarred its golden fur was. It looked as if it had been through terrible battles. No part of the huge cat seemed free of scars, which looked old and like they had been bad enough that the cat should not have lived.

The more he looked at the cat, the more Jack felt this suffering animal must be really old, and by old, he was thinking ancient. But something about this huge, impossible beast made Jack feel sorry for it. The tiger had almost stopped breathing by the time Jack stepped within eight feet. He really wanted to learn more about the cat, but Jack could not watch the huge beast suffer any longer. Turning toward the game trail that would lead him to the river and the cabin, he ran away.

As he ran, Jack wondered if the cat sensed he was toxic to it and that it should stay away. It seemed to be trying hard to get away from him after he changed his direction suddenly and got upwind of it.

He wished he had a camera to take a picture of the tiger so he could ask Bear if he had seen anything like it. Jack would certainly talk to Uncle Mick to see if he could learn anything about the ancient sabertoothed tiger in the forest. Thankful he didn't hear the sound of anything following him, Jack prayed he would never hear it again.

15

At the cabin, Jack went right to the computer, signed in, and began talking to Uncle Mick. Jack told Mick what he had encountered in the forest and asked, "Do you have any idea what a prehistoric sabertoothed tiger would be doing in an alpine forest?"

Jack was looking at Mick's face on the screen after he asked him what he knew of a huge cat, and he could swear Uncle Mick's computer program looked surprised and worried before it answered his questions.

"There is no such animal as you have described," said Uncle Mick's image in the monitor.

"But I can answer questions about unexplained sounds in the forest," continued Mick. "When I was running in the woods, something made sounds such as you described, but I was never able to get sight of it."

Then he shifted gears. "Jack, your sudden move crosswind when you turned ninety degrees to go around the fallen tree went undetected by the cat. It sounds as though it may find your smell more unpleasant than I did. There were times after you had a long workout, on a sweltering summer day when you were younger and less willing to bathe in the icy river, that I too felt sickened by your smell."

Without warning, the Mick in the program began to laugh, and as suddenly as he started, he stopped laughing.

With a straight face, Mick said, "Pardon the outburst. It was caused by faulty input done years ago. I just thought humor would help if you were younger when I passed." As Jack tried to process this, Mick said, "It won't happen again." Then he suggested that Jack head to town as soon as he could and talk to Bear. Mick told Jack to access him later and add any information he got from Bear into his database.

Jack stared at the screen in disbelief as the image suddenly said, "Goodbye." He could swear that the computer program was surprised by the information about the big cat. Mick had made a joke and closed the conversation rather than him closing it.

That was weird, Jack thought as the monitor went black. *How could Mick's program react to current information he had not before encountered? This computer is more advanced than I thought.*

Jack walked into the cabin's main room, looked at his watch, and saw it was just 11:00. He could drive into town to find Bear. First, he'd prepare for civilization by taking a quick bath in the river before going into town. Grabbing his towel and soap, he headed to the bathing hole.

The water was cold, and Jack took his bath in steps. Wading in as far as he could into the chilly water, he splashed himself and then soaped up. He threw the soap to the bank, took a deep breath, and dove under the freezing water to rinse the soap off. In seconds he came sputtering up and dashed to shore. The water had been so cold his teeth chattered. "Darn Mick for not putting in a shower," he said, determined to install a shower soon.

Jack dried off while walking back to the cabin. In minutes he was dressed, in the truck and headed into town. It was time to go see Bear. As he drove, Jack thought about Uncle Mick's computer program and how weird it seemed. Mick had said he had spent years recording various scenarios to cover every situation that might come up, but that couldn't be right. If he did not know of any such animal as the one Jack described, then why did he make a recording that covered something he knew nothing about? Mick's program was reacting almost human the way he looked concerned when it heard about the sabertoothed tiger and the way Mick had joked about his needing a bath. Jack was not a computer expert and could not be sure how advanced that program was, but he was determined to pay closer attention in the future to their conversations to see if he could observe more anomalies in the program.

He parked the truck up from the main road and walked the rest of the way. When he hit the trail that led to the back of the café, Jack turned and headed quietly into the kitchen and stood just inside the back door until Michelle came in from the front.

When she saw Jack, she smiled and gave him a hug. Jack held her tightly and let her go only when Bear walked into the kitchen.

Again, Jack and Michelle were caught. Bear said, "I told you once, Jack, not to mess with my lunch hour, and here you go doing it again." He laughed loudly and then came over to greet him.

After everyone else had greeted Jack, he said to Bear, "we need to talk."

"Sure," said Bear, glancing at the concerned look on Jack's face.

The others gathered around to quietly listen.

"What's wrong, Jack?"

While Michelle sat next to him, the story poured out of Jack—the run, the strange sound, the beast, the sighting of the giant saber-toothed tiger. When he got to the part where he described how he seemed to be toxic to the tiger, eyes widened, and the room got very still.

Jack looked around him at the questioning looks on faces in the room. He wondered if they thought he had lost it all alone up on the mountain.

When he was done, he asked Bear, "Have you ever heard of a big cat like that in any of the tribal history?"

The room was silent as they waited for at least five minutes before Bear began to speak. "Jack," Bear began, "There is text from the very beginning of our time that mentions big animals at this mountain. The texts say something about huge cats plaguing the land and the guardians before the Great Father chased them away. If you are indeed the reincarnation of the Great Father, Jack, then you may have the same effect on the huge cats that he did. He must have driven them off as you did today."

Shaking his head, Bear got up from the table, saying, "I must learn more about it." He added, "We will find the underlying cause of this mystery as quickly as possible, but now you and I must go back to the cabin. I have things to tell you. For now, they are for your ears only."

16

The drive up to Mick's cabin went by without a word. Jack knew Bear well enough not to talk until Bear was ready. Jack exited the truck and headed through the front door with Bear following. Once inside the cabin, Bear opened the new computer room door, walked inside, and waited for Jack to follow him before he closed the door. He approached the computer table and placed his palm on the tabletop. As soon as Bear placed his hand on the tabletop, the room was filled with noise, and hidden panels slid open all over the room, revealing new computer monitors.

Jack stared in disbelief as the room went from a single computer and monitor to a full-blown computer lab. Bear spoke for the first time since leaving the café. He looked at Jack and simply said, "Things have changed more around here than you could imagine. Jack, you don't know this, but Mick had more money than any other human on earth. He used some of it to build the best science labs in the world. Those labs have made breakthroughs here that are decades ahead of even top-secret government labs.

"Are you still wearing the watch Coach Sulli gave you?" asked Bear.

"Yes, why?"

"Jack, the watch Sulli gave you is not an ordinary watch. It is a one-of-a-kind prototype from one of Mick's top-secret labs. That watch has more functions than an air force fighter jet."

"What does that mean?"

Bear looked at Jack and said, "Jack, you have a device on your wrist that can perform most every scientific function imaginable. It can monitor the wearer's life signs, including advanced tests you normally go to a lab for. It contains radar, infrared scanning, and a full spectrum of communications, including voice and video. The glasses it comes with have a heads-up display that allows you to scan all the readings. It is so powerful that you can zoom in on a fly a mile away and see its wings as if it were inches from your face. The electronic scanning functions can tell you how far away something is, how fast it is going, and how big it is, including its weight. "Jack, since the minute you put it on your wrist, it has been recording every minute of every day using its sensors."

Jack gasped, looked at Bear, and said, "What?"

"Not to worry, Jack. It has not been transmitting anything except your GPS location. We had only planned to use it for a GPS locator just in case someone tried to kidnap you. Now, it looks as though we need the other functions," he said.

Bear told Jack the watch had a powerful computer that knew what part of the recordings it could and could not record or monitor. "That includes personal times like the bathroom times or dates with Michelle . . . so you do not have to worry about anyone seeing your private moments. As soon as you are in a highly personal situation, the watch's computer blocks all data from being sent to a monitoring and diagnostic computer receiver.

"Jack," said Bear, I need your permission to have all the data the watch sensors have recorded, downloaded and analyzed."

"Bear, is it really possible for the data to show pictures of that huge cat? Maybe you'll believe me then, and I can really believe it myself!"

"If you saw it, it should be recorded. Now, let's see if we can set the watch to download all its data. Then I'll set it to transmit all current data and any future data if you are OK with that," said Bear."

"Go for it, Bear." Bear held out his hand for the watch. Jack took off the watch and handed it to Bear, who took it over to one of the computer stations in the newly revealed lab and sat down. Bear placed the watch onto a metal plate next to the keyboard, and the computer monitor came to life. Bear typed in a command, then handed the watch back to Jack, saying, "Here, put this back on and never take it off until you are told to do so."

"Now, we will let the computer search the data and see what it produces." As Bear spoke, the computer monitor began flashing options, and Bear said, "Let's find out what you and the watch saw." He hit the view option and leaned back to watch.

Jack was astounded at the quality of the video that appeared on the screen and asked, "How can the video be so clear and detailed?"

Bear replied, "The video is not from a camera. It is from a beam like a laser that scans the area around the wearer in a full 360 degrees circle, and it has an almost unlimited range. When I said you could see a fly's wings from a mile away, I was understating its abilities by at least ten miles. The best feature is that you can zoom in with it in any direction with the same quality added."

Jack stared at the monitor and asked, "Can I download the video every night and study it myself?"

"Sure," said Bear, "but why?"

Jack couldn't take his eyes off the monitor. "By using the watch's abilities, I am hoping to get a glimpse of my guardian," Jack admitted. "I've always wanted to see what my guardian looks like, and now maybe I'll be able to."

"Could we do that later?" Bear asked as he was fast-forwarding to when Jack saw the sabertoothed tiger.

Jack said, "Sure. Set it to this morning around 9:30 a.m."

Bear put on a weird-looking headset with a small eye-loop in front of his right eye and sat back. Immediately, the images on the monitor started flashing by faster and faster. Jack was watching Bear's face and the monitor as the images went flying by and realized that Bear was controlling the monitor with his mind using the headset.

Jack knew the headset had to be a new piece of technology from Mick's lab and wanted to try it as soon as he could. He could only imagine how easy it would be to do homework and surf the web with it. And the watch could be an immense advantage during races. With the heads-up display, Jack could watch every opponent in the race without turning his head.

Then Jack thought about how Mick would rather he use his senses instead. Mick had taught Jack to tune into his environment and all living beings, and Jack used that in races to tell when his competitors were tiring. He listened to their breathing to hear if it was laboring and heard how hard their feet were hitting to see if their strides were shortening as they tired.

Bear's voice pulled him back to the present, and he looked up at the monitor in time to see the huge cat just as he did earlier that morning. Bear started laughing and cussing as he watched the big cat. Neither man spoke until the video showed Jack leaving the cat, and even then, it took both men a minute before they could talk.

"At least I wasn't seeing things," said Jack.

"I wouldn't have believed it if I hadn't seen it for myself," said Bear, shaking his head. "This cat should not exist," Bear said. "This specimen is bigger than the normal sabertoothed tiger that died out thousands of years ago. This is crazy! I cannot imagine why this super-sized cat is here. And what is making it get sick near you, Jack?

"Jack, we need to wait for the labs to finish reviewing the data the watch recorded. My guess is the labs will not get back to us until morning with the results of the analysis."

"What do you think is going on?" asked Jack.

"I really don't know," answered Bear. "There may be a connection between the big cats the Great Father dealt with and the one you have, but again it is just a guess at this point.

Jack looked up from the monitor and asked Bear, "Do you have any idea why the big cat has been following me if it makes him so sick?

"Jack, I have no idea what is going on around here, which is quite rare for me. Now, can you take me back to town? Looks like we'll need to deal with this in the morning. I have some research to do before I meet with you tomorrow."

The ride back to town was just as quiet as the one to the cabin. All Bear said as he got out of the truck was, "Jack, I know you want to talk to Michelle, but please get some rest tonight, and I will see you at 7:30 in the morning at the Last Stop."

As Bear walked away, Jack got out of the truck and headed to the café. As he entered the restaurant, he was hit hard fast and was totally wrapped up in Michelle's arms as the sound of laughter filled the room. Finally, Michelle released her python grip on Jack and stepped back.

"I know it has only been hours, but I was worried about you after your run-in with the tiger."

Jack held Michelle at arm's length and smiled into her worried dark eyes. "I'm OK and plan to stay that way."

Seeing that the others in the café seemed to be waiting to hear a report from him, he said, "Let me have something to eat first, and I'll tell you what I know." Michelle was already in the kitchen before Jack finished his sentence.

Before Jack could finish saying hello to everyone in the restaurant, Michelle came out of the kitchen with her arms loaded with his meal. It didn't take long for him to finish eating, as he knew they were all waiting for him to speak.

He stood and began, "You've all probably heard something followed me on my morning run. On first look at it, it appeared to be a giant tiger. Bear was able to verify that it, indeed, was a saber-toothed tiger. That's disturbing enough on its own, but even more interesting is that this one is larger than any known extinct ones.

"The runner's watch given to me to test also takes and records video and it captured the incident with the giant cat. At this time, a lab is analyzing the recordings and will verify the information. Hopefully, they'll be able to give us an answer as to how it can be alive and what it is doing here."

When Jack stopped and looked around the room, Michelle broke in and asked, "Jack, do you feel safe with that huge tiger hunting you?"

"Thanks for worrying about me," he said. Then, looking at the still worried Michelle but addressing everyone in the café, he said, "Everyone, please remember that the cat was trying to get away from me. When I got too close, it got sick and looked like it was going to die. I think it was following me for a reason, but it knew it could not get too close. When I turned unexpectedly into the woods, I must have caught it off guard, got too close and that made the cat sick. Bear's best bet is that cat will not try getting close to me again anytime soon."

Michelle looked at Jack and said, "If that thing kills you, I will hurt you so bad, Jack, you won't sleep for a week."

The room erupted with laughter. It took a while to quiet down before Jack could finish his talk.

"I don't have anything more to add until we hear back from the lab tomorrow. Bear will meet me here at 7:30 for breakfast, and we will go over the lab results. Anyone who would like to listen to the results, please know you are all welcome. We are a family, and we will not have any secrets. Anything you want to know is just a question away."

As chairs scraped back and people said their good-byes and headed out, Jack turned to Michelle, took her hands in his, looked her in the eyes, and said, "Michelle, I promise not to do anything that endangers my life in any way." Then he jokingly added, "Mostly out of fear you would kill me if I got hurt like you said."

Then he headed out the back door and onto the path leading to his truck and the cabin in the woods.

17

The next morning the weather was clear and still cool at 6:30 a.m. when Jack hit the trail on his run to town. All the animals in the forest stayed away, so the woods were quiet as he ran. He listened carefully for any evidence of the sabertoothed tiger, but all was quiet.

In town, Jack jogged to Michelle's house to grab a shower before the meeting with Bear in twenty minutes. Michelle left a note saying she was at the café working on breakfast and would have a cup of coffee waiting for him when he arrived.

Jack walked into a full room in the café at 7:15. A chorus of "Good morning!" rang out from around the room as he made his way to where Bear was sitting. Bear had a briefcase in front of him on the table and an impatient look on his face as if he had been waiting.

When he saw Jack, he stood, picked up the briefcase, and said, "We need to leave right away."

"Where to?" Jack asked, his stomach rumbling.

"I'll tell you on the way."

Just then, Michelle came out of the kitchen with a large to-go box.

Jack followed Bear out the back door through the kitchen, where a small 4x4 Jeep was waiting. They hopped in the Jeep, and Bear said, "We're headed to one of Mick's labs."

At a clearing up the mountain a few miles, Bear stopped at a helicopter pad where one waited, looking like something out of a sci-fi movie.

Bear introduced Jack to the pilot, Kent, also a member of their tribe. Kent shook hands and said, "Good to meet you, Jack. I'm always at your disposal if needed."

Then he gave Jack a quick tour of the incredible craft. "First, regardless of what Bear says, this is not a helicopter but an electric-powered supersonic drone. It can take off vertically and accelerate to over five times the speed of sound without a sonic boom. The best part is this bird is invisible to radar and thermal imaging due to the built-in skin cooling needed for high speeds. The cooling system can keep the skin temperature the same as the air around it, making it invisible to thermal cameras."

As the men climbed in for takeoff, Jack found the inside of the drone just as incredible as the outside. With no visible windows inside, every wall looked as though it were made of transparent glass. The instrument panels were built-in flat-screen monitors, and the piloting controls were built like video game joystick controllers. Kent pointed out that the
rotors were built like ducted fans.

Seeing Jack was totally blown away by the advanced technology he was seeing, Bear turned to Jack with a grin. "This level of development is decades ahead of the rest of the world, Lobo. There is much for you to learn about the advancements we have made—and much of it is more incredible than this drone."

Kent added, "There are designs faster than this one and ones that can go into orbit."

Jack and Bear took a seat on either side of Kent and strapped in. The seats were similar to a recliner but with five-point seat restraints. Jack assumed the restraints were because of the high speeds and kept looking around.

Kent asked, "Everyone strapped in and ready for take-off?"

Bear and Jack had barely answered, "Yes," when the drone rose into the air so smoothly it was unnoticeable without looking through the transparent walls.

The drone rose quickly and started forward simultaneously. Within a couple minutes, Kent said the drone was at 1,000 feet, cruising at Mach 6. Jack could not fathom how this drone could gain height and speed so quickly, with him barely feeling any acceleration.

He asked Kent, who said the drone had an inertia-dampening field generator. "Simply put," he said, "anything inside the field bubble feels no acceleration. The field contains all the molecules within the drone as if they were a solid block. This means each molecule inside the field moves as one, producing an area where there is no movement. This allows the craft to accelerate and maneuver at any speed without harming anyone or anything inside."

Kent looked over at Bear, who was looking up at the clouds and asked, "Do we have time to show Lobo a cool feature of the drone?"

Bear got a big smile on his face and said, "At your command."

With that, the drone tilted slightly back and went up. It went up so far that they were in outer space in seconds.

"Jack," asked Kent, "Do you want to try weightlessness?"

Seconds later, Jack was unstrapped and floating weightless.

"Swimming doesn't even come close to this," he said as he did a summersault.

"Look out the window to see what happens when the drone accelerates," said Kent. He put the drone through fast maneuvers, and Jack did not feel a thing. He kept floating as if they were not changing direction.

With his years of studying science, Jack could hardly believe he was not being thrown around by inertia.

Kent said, "You'll have the opportunity to ask the scientists about any of this new technology. Mick always had regular briefings so he could keep up with the latest." Then Kent said, "Go ahead and strap back in before we enter gravity unless you like falling."

Jack hurried to do so before the drone dropped back into the atmosphere and continued its high-speed trip to the lab.

The drone had slowed down and dropped into a valley between two mountain peaks. Bear said, "Jack, look to your left at the cliff face below."

Up ahead on the face of the cliff, an opening began to appear in the rock face. Soon it was big enough for them to fly through. Kent guided the drone into the opening with the precision of a surgeon. The small opening became a large cavern once inside. The drone landed between half a dozen other similar crafts and others of assorted sizes and designs.

As they disembarked, Jack stared at the high-tech equipment in the secret hanger. Bear grinned and said, "Follow and do not touch."

Kent laughed, shook Jack's hand, "I'll always be at your disposal; contact me when you need me. Or if you want to go play sometime too."

Jack followed Bear across the hanger to a door with a sign saying Complex 37 Bio-Tech.

He thought, *If this is Complex #37, there must be thirty-six more someplace.* He followed Bear through the door and down a long hall with doors at intervals.

Without slowing, Bear said, "Behind each door is a separate lab. Each lab is working on a different problem or experiment. There are over 100 separate complexes like this hidden around the world. Each complex researches a different subject or problem. This lab specializes in bio- enhancements for humans, and that is why we are here."

Bio-enhancements? What do we need bio-enhancements for? Jack wondered.

After about what Jack figured was half a mile straight into the center of the mountain, Bear stopped at a door with a sign that read **AI-Enhanced Bio-Fusion.**

Jack was starting to feel overwhelmed and on edge, wondering what it had to do with him.

Bear seemed to sense Jack was uncomfortable and said, "Don't worry. We're just getting you fitted for a running suit."

"A running suit?"

"Yes," said Bear, a man of few words.

They walked through the door and into a lab the size of a basketball court filled with an incredible array of equipment and computers. There were eight people gathered around a large monitor across the room, which Bear headed over to, with Jack following right behind. As they approached, Jack could see the group was so engrossed in watching something they hadn't noticed them approaching.

When he finally got close enough to see what was on the monitor, he froze. They were looking at an image of a giant sabertoothed tiger. Jack was quite sure it was *his* tiger—the one he had encountered in the forest.

The first person to notice Jack and Bear walk up seemed startled and gave a yelp as he jumped. Bear started laughing and said, "Sorry for the scare. It's just me and Jack." They had been totally fixated on Jack's big cat and weren't aware they had walked in.

A man stepped forward and greeted them.

"Hi, Doctor Wiles," said Bear, "this fine young man is Jack."

Doc Wiles held out a hand to Jack and said, "Wonderful to meet you. Thank you for giving us the chance to view this specimen." As they shook hands, Doc Wiles said, "After seeing how you reacted during your encounter with this beast, young man, it is hard to tell if you are the bravest or craziest human I have ever met. I was seriously scared myself just watching the video in the lab."

Jack looked down and said, "I was terrified . . . until the cat started acting sick, then I felt sorry for it."

"Well," said Doc Wiles, "after analyzing the information from your watch, I can tell you that giant cat was up to no good."

"What do you mean?" asked Jack. "The cat seemed to want to get away."

"Step over to the monitor and let me show you what we found," said Doc Wiles. "We've analyzed the data from the watch starting with your first run on the mountain. What we've found has made us very worried."

Doc Wiles had an assistant pull up a program on the monitor and said, "Did you know that the sabertoothed tiger was stalking you every time you ran?"

Jack looked at Doc Wiles and asked, "What do you mean every time?"

Doc Wiles said, "We ran computer simulations all night before we produced a plausible reason why the sabertoothed tiger wanted to stalk you every time you ran. Look at the results.

Motioning for someone to start the video, he said, "What we are about to watch is a short sequence from each run you have taken. We've edited out the sections where you were alone, leaving only the parts that have the big cat in them."

Jack watched the footage, fascinated and feeling a bit weird by being observed by everyone.

Doc Wiles said, "In the beginning, the big cat did not get close. It may have been too far away for you to hear it. But as the days progressed, the cat began coming closer until you accidentally surprised it by cutting into the woods. From its reaction to your proximity, your scent or pheromones are poison to it."

After ten minutes of watching short clips of the cat following him, Jack shook his head and said, "That creeps me out. What do you think is going on?"

"Here's what I think, "said Doc Wiles. "The cat appeared to be trying to become acclimated to your poison. The way it would come close, then back off after it got shaky, then come close again may mean it is trying to become immune to you.

"Why?" asked Jack.

"Not sure," said Doc Wiles, "but it can't be for any good reason. Worst-case scenario, it wants to kill you! We obviously can't let that happen, so we have a plan. We've developed a suit that completely covers your body, except for your face. The suit will contain your pheromones and stop the cat from becoming immune to you."

"Really, Doc? A one-piece running suit? How am I expected to run in long johns?

"Oh, I think you will like the suit. It won't be as bad to wear as you think. There are features you will appreciate."

Doc Wiles got up and said, "Please follow me."

18

Jack followed Doc Wiles through a door in the back of the lab into another training gym filled with sophisticated electronic exercise equipment that made his college gym's equipment look like it came out of the Dark Ages.

Doc Wiles saw the look of surprise on Jack's face and said, "Anytime you want to do a little training on these machines, we'd enjoy putting you through your paces."

"Absolutely, yes!"

"Check out the treadmill," said Doc Wiles. They walked to the corner where a massive treadmill about ten feet wide and twenty feet long stood.

The first thing Jack said was, "You could use this thing for relay baton passing practice, it's so long!"

Doc Wiles smiled and said, "Once you have your suit on, you can try it out on the treadmill."

"Alright, let's do it!"

Doc Wiles asked one of the lab workers to take Jack into the dressing room where the suit was and get him outfitted.

Jack and the lab worker returned after twenty minutes, and Jack fully suited up in a dark full body covering.

"How does it feel?" asked Doc Wiles.

"It feels fantastic, it has no weight at all—almost as if I had no clothes on."

"Great," Doc Wiles said, "now it's time to put it through the paces to see how well it works."

He motioned Jack over to the giant treadmill. Another lab assistant had him start stretching and prepare to do his warmup jogging on the treadmill. While Jack began his stretching routine, Bear and Doc Wiles stood next to the treadmill watching.

"How's your hearing with the hood up?" asked the doc.

"Sounds good—just like I have earbuds in. Everything is perfectly clear and sounds like it is right next to me, even if it is across the lab."

"That's because that suit has a complete audio system," said Doc Wiles.

"How is that possible?" Jack said, his hand running over the hood. "I can't feel any wires or speakers."

As Jack continued his warmup, Doc Wiles asked the lab assistant to go over the basic operating functions of the suit with him.

"How can a thin lycra suit have operating functions?" asked Jack.

Bear, who was watching carefully, said, "I thought this suit was designed to block Jack's pheromones.

"Oh, it does block them," said the assistant, "but not simply by locking them in. This suit filters out the pheromones, so a little can be released or all of it. It's computer controlled and advanced beyond anything you have ever seen or imagined. The suit can change its shape, rigidity, color, control internal and external temperatures, and so much more. Most importantly, the suit syncs with your mental and physical functions—your neural system. When it begins monitoring the information, it is sent to this lab for processing and analysis."

Jack, who was still warming up, had a puzzled look on his face. "How's that possible?"

"To be perfectly honest, we don't know all the abilities of the suit," the assistant said.

"Why not?"

"The suit is a highly-advanced artificial intelligence computer, and it has been building and rebuilding itself over the last year as it continues to learn.

"So . . . the suit itself is a computer?"

"Not just a computer, an artificial-intelligence computer," the assistant said. "The AI suit can alter itself, and in various situations, even the person wearing it, to control and protect. The original suit was designed to protect soldiers during battle situations and can stop bullets or lasers."

Doc Wiles said, "The suit's ability to protect you on its own is why it was chosen for you."

As Jack finished his stretches and started a slow jog on the treadmill, he asked, "How fast can this treadmill go, Doc?"

"Not sure, Jack, its speed is controlled by the suit. The suit reacts to the instructions sent by your brain to your body. In other words, the suit links with your brain and changes the speed on the treadmill depending on how fast you want to run at that moment.

"If you were running at a constant pace, then wanted to do a sprint, the suit would send a message to the treadmill and change its speed at the exact moment of your decision. The result is the treadmill feels exactly like running on a solid, unmoving surface. If you fall, the treadmill will stop instantly."

"How on earth can a cloth suit could be so powerful?" asked Jack, shaking his head.

Doc Wiles said, "The suit is not made from cloth, but carbon atom nanotubes that make Buckminsterfullerene or Buckyballs. Out of those, we made what we call Bucky Cloth, which is ten times lighter than steel yet 500 times stronger. Once Bucky Cloth was developed, the AI computer was integrated into its structure. The finished product is a self-aware computer that can protect you against most emergencies. It can change shape if needed. That function allows it to move independently as, or when, needed."

Blown by the suit's capabilities, Jack lightened the moment by asking, "Can it run for me while I take a nap?"

With a chuckle, the assistant said, "Not while napping, but it can run the suit itself if you want."

"How do you get the suit to run on its own?" Jack asked. Just then, he felt the suit start making jerky pushing and pulling motions.

The assistant said, "It's adjusting on its own. Relax and think about running naturally."

As Jack relaxed, his sensory input to the suit increased, and the less Jack needed to exert himself. After three of four minutes, Jack said, "It feels like I'm not putting any effort into running, the suit's doing it all!"

Doc Wiles turned to Bear and said, "I've never seen the suit and an operator synchronize so quickly."

The lab assistant chimed in, "This suit-to-human sync is not only the fastest but the strongest I've observed. It usually takes days for a subject to successfully have the control Jack is showing."

Doc Wiles looked at Jack and asked him, "Do you feel like your body is ready for a sprint?"

Jack smiled and the treadmill began to spin faster as his strides increased in length and speed. Within seconds Jack was sprinting on the treadmill and his smile was getting bigger.

He looked over at Bear while sprinting and asked, while not breathing harder than if he were jogging, "It wouldn't be legal to race in this suit, but I can see how it could help paralyzed people walk!"

Bear asked, "Are you doing any of the running?"

"Not a bit. I feel like I could almost go to sleep, it's so automatic. All I'm doing is thinking about running and the suit does exactly what I am thinking!"

Doc Wiles asked Jack to slow down and stop running and asked, "How are you feeling?"

"Great. It felt as though I was not moving my legs, but they were being moved by the suit. Not sure how the Bucky Cloth can move my legs without any physical effort from me. It's fantastic."

The lab assistants and Jack spent the next five hours reviewing the suit's incredible features.

The lab had designed a considerable number of abilities, but the suit had designed and built into itself other capabilities. Early in its development, the suit showed signs of being self-aware. It was making decisions and changes the lab had no control over. Furthermore, the suit would only let them know limited information about the changes it had made.

The assistant said, "The suit can transform itself into almost any shape. Just for fun, imagine you have a shark's fin on your back."

After some effort, Jack was able to make the suit transform the back into a shark's fin. The assistant laughed and began producing different transformations like flippers and angel wings, and even changing the hardness of each one.

Jack's favorite was when he made the suit into a big bubble with his head sticking out the top and got it to bounce like a ball.

After playing with the suit for a while, Jack and the lab assistant practiced using the suit functions needed to keep him safe from the sabertoothed tiger. The lab machines measured his pheromones released into the air while he controlled the suit and tried running on the treadmill.

In the event of an attack by the giant cat, they had Jack insert his arm into a machine that simulated being crushed or bitten. He learned how to make the suit hard and bulletproof.

When the lab assistant felt Jack had become sufficiently adept at controlling the suit, he brought out the glasses that went with his watch. The glasses had heads-up displays in both lenses, allowing Jack to view everything his watch picked up. He could zoom, photograph, X-ray, and thermal image with them. Jack could have his speed, distance, direction, and rear- or side- facing camera all projected onto the lenses.

The watch and glasses were Jack's favorite. As he practiced, he thought of how they could help during a race. After almost five hours of wearing the suit, Jack still could hardly tell it was on. It was not too tight or too loose, not too warm or cold, but fit perfectly, like a second skin.

"There's something else," the assistant said. "You can wear the suit 24/7."

"What do you mean?"

With a slight smile, the assistant said, "The suit is self-cleaning.

Not only the outside and inside of the suit but it will also clean your body. To take care of any bodily functions, all you need to do is instruct the suit to open in the front or back and go as usual. Plus, in an emergency, if you were unconscious and had an accident inside the suit, the suit would clean you and itself."

Jack laughed, saying, "I hope that never happens, but glad it can take care of it if it does."

"Wear the suit all the time," the assistant said, "especially on the mountain." He could take it off when showering or in personal situations, but with the potential dangers lurking since he became Mick's heir, he said keeping it on was safer.

The last thing Jack learned was how to alter the suit to look like regular clothes, even losing the hood, so it wouldn't be noticeable in normal situations.

When Jack met up with Doc Wiles and Bear later, the doc asked, "Do you feel comfortable operating the suit, or do you need more training?"

"Totally. Everything was great. I look forward to trying these new toys in the real world!"

Bear made a joke about Jack being such a child and only wanting the toys. Doc Wiles laughed, shook Jack's hand, and said, "I think you will be fine, Lobo."

19

"Are you hungry, Jack?" Bear asked as they walked out the door and down the long hall.

"Starved, Bear. How did you know?" After all those hours in the lab being trained on the suit, Jack could eat.

He and Bear found the cafeteria with its waiting buffet filled with hot and cold foods, salads, desserts, and round tables in an attractive, brightly lit room.

The two filled their plates and ate quickly as Bear said they had one more stop.

After lunch, they walked down the hall and entered another double door into another room filled with computers and lab equipment. A gray-haired lady saw the two as they came in and walked over to greet them.

"Hello, Bear," she said, then turned to Jack, still outfitted in his new suit, and smiled, "Hi, Jack, I am Dr. Ellen. Please come with me, you two, we are having a brainstorming session about the best way to deal with this sabertoothed tiger of Lobo's."

Surprised she had used his nickname, Jack knew she must be another tribal member. Dr. Ellen led them to a conference table with a dozen people sitting around it, watching the sabertoothed tiger on a large monitor.

Dr. Ellen interrupted by clearing her throat loudly and saying, "Jack and Bear are here." Some in the group looked up, clearly startled. Bear laughed as everyone regained their composure. Once the group settled down, everyone said hello and introduced themselves.

Dr. Ellen asked the computer operator to start the video from the beginning so they could all watch it together. As they watched the video, the group members gave observations of what they thought the big cat was trying to accomplish. Most came to the same conclusion —the cat was trying to build up a tolerance to Jack.

Dr. Ellen agreed and asked Bear about the tests Doc Wiles had run on Jack. Bear replied, "The tests could not identify anything out of normal parameters. Jack is in top physical conditioning." Bear told the group, "Doc Wiles theorizes it may be Jack's pheromones making the cat sick."

"Sounds reasonable," said Dr. Ellen, "and the suit would be perfect to mask it." She then asked the group for their opinions and suggestions on how to proceed. The group was unanimous about the pheromones and using the suit for containment.

"Now we must produce a plan to implement containment without the sabertoothed tiger knowing," said Dr. Ellen. "This big cat should not exist, but it does, and it is highly intelligent, so we must use great caution."

She wanted them to consider every danger that could possibly arise. Two hours later, the consensus was to slowly decrease the percentage of pheromones the suit released so the big cat would not notice. The cat would continue getting closer for longer periods of time, thinking it was becoming immune.

Then Dr. Ellen asked, "Has a time been established for when the big cat would be immune enough to enable it to hurt Jack before he accidentally made it sick?

One team member drew attention to the monitor. He said, "Based on the cat's previous pattern of close encounters with Jack, our calculations estimate between six and eight weeks from now. We have also concluded the cat would die from any encounter close enough for it to hurt Jack. Since the cat got extremely ill from the last encounter, we figure it was sick enough to set the cat back weeks."

A tech sitting beside him said, "Due to the big cat's decreased immunity, Jack's suit will be set at 50 percent pheromone containment the first day back on the mountain, and the cat should not notice. Start with the suit at 50 percent, then decrease it to 10 percent a week until the suit is at 10 percent. We recommend a one-and-a-half percent decrease per day, which gives us the 10 percent decrease per week required. Jack will have the suit at 10 percent in four weeks. Computer simulations show that at 90 percent containment, the sabertoothed tiger cannot gain immunity regardless of how long or close to Jack it gets. If it were within twenty feet of Jack after the four-week period, when the suit opened to one hundred percent, the cat would perish."

As the group finalized the plan, Bear and Jack left the room. Bear stopped at an office door down the hall and said, "There's someone else I want you to talk with, Jack."

When he entered the room, Jack saw a short man sitting at a desk inputting data at his computer. Engrossed in his work, it took a while before he realized Bear and Jack were in the room. When he looked up and noticed Bear, he smiled deeply, walked over and hugged Bear.

Jack thought it was an odd sight to see this little man hugging huge Bear. Bear detached himself from the man and motioned Jack forward. Jack stepped forward as the little man looked at him with a surprised look. Bear said, "Jack, this is Jeff, who does our communications."

As Jeff offered his hand to Jack, Bear said, "Jeff, it's time Jack played an active part in our plans."

Jack had a confused look on his face, but Bear just chuckled and said, "It's time to let Jack know what the announcement is going to be about."

Jeff shrugged his shoulders and said, "As you may have guessed, I am another tribal member. My job is press secretary for all the tribe's companies and dealing with all the government communications and interactions. Bear wants me to inform you of the announcement we are making to the world today."

"What announcement?" asked Jack, giving Jeff a blank look.

Jeff picked up a small remote, turned toward a screened wall, activated the remote, and the screen lit up with a world map full of brightly-lit dots.

He said, "Jack, we have planned to offer this technology to the world for a long time, but the political climate has not been good enough until now. Since the treaties will also be ending soon, we now have something to sweeten the bargain and cushion the blow."

At the mention of "cushion the blow," Jack gave his full attention to the little man with the remote as the screen changed from a map to a picture of a huge ship.

Jeff said, "This ship, a freighter, and over one hundred more just like it, is about to change the world as we know it."

Jeff smiled at Jack's confused look and said, "These ships were your Uncle Mick's biggest dream. Mick wanted to bring access to fresh, clean water to the world. He knew that climate change would only make the drought worldwide worse and wanted to help. He spent years researching the problem and then put billions into the solution. It took another few years to get governments around the world to allow us to implement the program. Not all the governments wanted us in their countries with this kind of technology until we convinced them to let us."

"Convinced, ha!" said Bear. "Convinced is another way of saying we extorted them."

"Oh, well, yes, we kind of did," interjected Jeff, "but they soon saw the reason behind our program."

Bear looked at Jack and said, "What Jeff is saying is, we knew what their governments had done. We said we would let the world know about some things they do not want known, so they gave us clearance to launch the programs—that is with their supervision, of course . . . not that they can do anything once it starts anyway."

'Once it starts?' What does Bear mean by that? Jack listened carefully as Jeff continued, wondering how it all fits with him.

"The ship you are looking at is technologically the most advanced piece of manufactured machinery ever constructed. It's twice the size of any ship ever built, and that is just the beginning. Inside, it's a floating factory containing fifty smaller identical factories ready to be launched once a ship reaches its destination.

"At their destinations, each ship will anchor, then begin drawing materials from the ocean floor and the sea water. As it approaches land, it will mine materials it needs from the land along the way."

Jack couldn't wait another second. He interrupted with, "But, what are they making? What's the end product?"

"Those fifty small factories are water-making factories," said Jeff. "Once each factory is launched, it will first duplicate itself, then each duplicate will duplicate itself until they have made ten copies. Once all copies are made, each factory will begin building a water pipeline while it travels inland to where the water is needed.

"Jack, it is estimated that the factory ships will produce enough water so even drought-starved Africa will have enough excess water to refill all the inland seas and create an oasis out of their deserts.

"Mick's dream was made possible because of the nanotechnology we created in our labs. That technology is the missing link required to build self-replicating machines. Once the first programed nano-robot is created, it builds identical nano-bots, then soon, you have a small army doing your bidding.

"Our bidding this time is to build thousands of miles of water pipeline and solar pumping stations so water can be delivered anywhere you need it. These pipelines will be underground, so they will not have an impact on the ecology and preserve the natural land-scape. Each pipeline will build small lakes as they progress, and these lakes will be water reservoirs. Areas of the globe suffering from terrible drought where rivers, lakes, and seas have dried up will be full again. Populated areas will have extra lakes for storage and recreation. No human or animal will ever have to worry about water again. Incredibly—the best part is the pipelines will be completed in approximately two weeks."

"Two weeks?" asked Jack. "You are going to build thousands of miles of pipeline, thousands of pumping stations, and thousands of lakes in two weeks across the globe?"

Jeff looked at Jack with a totally serious face and said emphatically, "Yes! Jack, this plan will work. In two weeks, every person on earth will, for the first time in recorded history, have enough clean water to meet their needs. Unlimited clean, fresh water is just the beginning." He waved his arm and said, "There's more . . . We will talk later of other plans Mick had in process."

Jack shook his head, amazed at what he had just heard when Bear said, "We've got a drone to catch. It's time to go home."

The two men walked down the long hallway to the hanger where pilot Kent had been summoned to fly them home. Jack's head was spinning with all he had learned about the changes to come.

He thought about the sabertoothed tiger lurking in the forest and the suit he was now wearing. *Will it really work to keep me safe?*

20

The drone ride home was quiet and uneventful. Jack was in such deep thought he hardly noticed time passing. It was after 11:00 p.m. when they arrived at the clearing where the Jeep was parked.

As Bear drove the road to the cabin to drop Lobo off, he looked at the quiet young man beside him. He said, "Quite a day, huh?" Then without waiting, he said, "Maybe we should go over a few things before I leave you.

"First thing is never take that suit off while outside the cabin. We can't take a chance on the big cat figuring out what we have done using the suit, so please be careful. The suit is pre-programed to adjust the pheromone level each day, so you won't have to do that. The lab will continuously monitor the suit's data and inform you of any situation that may be of concern. The glasses that link with the suit will allow you to monitor the suit and your body functions. And Jack, you are going to especially enjoy the video functions."

As Bear talked, Jack imagined the fun it would be to use glasses capable of seeing behind him and zooming in on things miles away.

"By the look on your face, you are not too upset about running in the suit and using the tech that goes with it," said Bear, smiling.

"The tech is great," Jack said. "I was worried about being too hot in the suit, but the suit can cool or heat depending on my needs. The suit does so many things it'll probably take weeks for me to try out even a small percentage of what it is capable of." He laughed and said, "You can bet I am going to try swimming in the river with it to see if it keeps me warm."

At the cabin, Bear asked when he'd see Jack next. Jack let him know his running schedule and that he would be down the next day after a short run.

"Please tell Michelle I will be there early enough for breakfast," said Jack.

Bear was half a mile down the road toward town before he stopped laughing about Jack's stomach.

Jack stood outside on the deck in the cool night air, thinking about the day and how his life had changed in four weeks. Life was more complicated than ever with all the changes, new information, and added responsibilities, but he didn't feel too stressed.

He thought about how Mick would have said it was his years of training keeping him calm, and Jack had to agree. Tomorrow he would take a dawn run with his full gear to see if he could attract the sabertoothed tiger. Even the thought of encountering the big cat did not stress him out. It wasn't just the protective suit, Jack felt sorry for the cat and wanted to keep it from being hurt.

Inside the cabin, he pulled off the suit and was surprised at how clean and not sweaty he felt. The lab tech had said the suit would keep him cool, warm, and clean, but he hadn't expected his skin would feel smooth and smell fresh after twelve hours in the suit.

Jack felt so good in the suit he went to bed in it to save time in the morning. He knew the next few weeks were going to be the real test of its cleaning abilities during his hard runs on hot days.

* * *

In the morning, Jack lay awake thinking about the strange dreams that plagued him all night long. After his family died two years earlier, he had experienced nightmares, but these dreams were different and weird.

It was as though someone had been talking to him in his dreams. Then again, not like someone, but *something* was talking—almost as if a child were asking him simple questions. Jack felt as if he had spent the whole night in his dreams tutoring a child about life and the world. Physically, his body felt great, but mentally he felt drained.

Good thing today's running is going to be easy, he thought, *no brain power involved*.

Strangely, he was not hungry as usual, but he made a protein shake. Dressing took no time at all, as it just meant putting on his shoes. He considered seeing if the suit could produce some shoes but decided to wait.

Outside, Jack put the new glasses on and synced them to his watch. Once the heads-up display flashed ready, he scanned the outside area around the cabin out of curiosity rather than concern about his safety. There was nothing dangerous detected inside the quarter-mile radius he scanned, so off he went on his run.

Today he would do a long slow run. For the first six miles, he would run near the cabin to see if he could attract the big cat. The lab had the suit set to 100 percent open in the event the cat got close enough to hurt Jack.

As he ran, Jack didn't feel at all scared, simply curious about the sabertoothed tiger. How was it possible for that beast to even exist? And why was he poisonous to it?

Just then, his glasses flashed a warning about something large moving toward him in the trees. It had to be the big cat! He did not need the heads-up display to tell him his heart rate had increased. He didn't feel scared, just excited. His heart rate increased until he could hear and feel it beating hard in his chest.

When the animal came into view, the display showed it was matching Jack's pace, just running slightly behind but slowly moving closer. The wind direction was toward the cat. Obviously, it was trying to get into the air flow that had blown over Jack's body, to get into his pheromones.

The tiger was running about seventy-five feet away when it began to stumble a bit. After a couple hundred more feet of running with Jack, the big cat turned and ran away from him.

Jack replayed the encounter and watched how the cat increasingly stumbled as it got closer until, finally, it broke away and ran off. The cat seemed sicker and unable to get as close to Jack since their first accidental meeting.

Amazingly, the suit was holding back 50 percent of his pheromones. The lab would soon have the data he had just recorded and analyze it. Jack felt sad about the cat getting sick but also safe, knowing the thing still could not get too close.

He finished running the loop around the cabin, then headed down the road to town, thinking, as usual, about Michelle—and one of her big breakfasts.

Jack slipped in the back door of the café and waved at the mid-morning crowd as he made his way over to Bear.

"Hey, look at that impressive new running outfit," someone complemented.

Jack looked at Bear and said, "Watch!" He then made the suit form small angel wings and flapped them as he walked around the dining room. The people gasped aloud as the suit transformed. Michelle came out of the kitchen, saw the wings, and said, "No way is that boy an angel!"

A chorus of laughter followed Jack. When things calmed down, Bear and Jack talked about the functions of the new suit and the long day they had testing it at the lab. They talked about the plan to lure the sabertoothed tiger in with hopes of trapping it once it had been subdued.

When she heard this, Michelle looked like she was about to have a heart attack. But Jack assured her the suit was more than capable of protecting him if the big cat got too close.

To prove it, he asked her for a big kitchen knife and stabbed the arm of his suit with it. It sounded like metal hitting metal as the knife bounced off. Then he took a heavy cast-iron pan and hit his knee as hard as he could. The sound was like two frying pans hitting.

"I didn't feel a thing," he said. "The suit absorbed every bit of the force."

Michelle was unhappy they were using Jack as bait but felt better knowing the suit was such good protection.

"What about those wings the suit made?" hollered out one of the guys.

Jack explained the suit could be transformed in ways other than becoming bulletproof hard. He showed them the shark fin and other changes he had tried before, and everyone gasped and laughed.

"I'm not sure how often I will need to transform the suit, but it sure is fun playing," Jack said.

"Nothing like giving an incredible tool to a boy who just wants to play dress-up," teased Michelle.

The room erupted in laughter when two hands emerged from Jack's suit and reached toward Michelle, grabbed her, and started tickling her. Michelle almost cried from laughing so hard before the hands stopped and disappeared back into the suit.

"Jack could tickle the big cat into submission if all else fails," said Bear.

Suddenly someone sent a muffin flying straight toward Jack, in a direct line at his face. Even Jack was surprised when it stopped just six inches short of its target. Looking down, he saw the suit had sent a thin cord of fabric out, which caught it. All eyes were on the muffin frozen in place. Jack had an idea, and the cord curled toward his mouth. Jack took a bite and said, "Thanks, Michelle."

"Figures," she said, "all he thinks about is eating."

"I think about running too," said Jack, and another muffin was launched with the same result.

Before people left, Bear and Jack informed everyone about the plan, and they seemed satisfied Jack would be safe. Bear reminded them once again to keep their eyes open for strangers and things out of the ordinary.

When it was only Bear, Michelle, and Jack left in the café, Bear asked her, "Are you honestly satisfied that we can keep Lobo safe?"

She took Jack's hand and looked deeply into his eyes, her eyes speaking volumes without a word being spoken. Then she said, "I know you are safe, Jack, but make doubly sure when you are out there to use those tools. Your life is more important than that cat's."

Jack gave Michelle a long hug, leaned back and said, "I promise."

She stepped back and gave Jack a strange double-take, looking him up and down. Then she looked at Bear with a questioning look. "Bear, am I imagining it or has Lobo grown taller overnight?"

"What?" Bear asked. "I don't notice any difference. But then I don't spend my spare time hugging Lobo like some people seem to do."

Jack looked down at Michelle and realized she was right. Either she had gotten shorter, or he was taller than usual next to her. Jack laughed and dismissed the thought. "Maybe the suit makes me seem taller."

Michelle said, "It must be my good cooking that's making this guy grow," and went into the kitchen to make Jack a hot plate of food while the guys talked.

Bear headed out, saying, "Keep both eyes open out there, Jack."

Michelle and Jack spent a couple of hours together before she had to get lunch ready.

"Unless you want to work, maybe you should head back to the cabin and get that plan complete, so I won't have to worry." She picked up a to-go box with a sandwich for his lunch as they walked out the back door and handed it to Jack.

Jack gave her a big smile and said, "Thanks!" He took the box and put it behind his back. When his hand came back around, it was empty.

Michelle looked at his empty hands and asked, "Have you already eaten it?"

With a gleam in his eye, Jack turned around to show her a net the suit had formed that was now holding the to-go box at his back. "I have been planning to try this since they showed me how to transform the suit."

She laughed and gave him a hug before he headed up the mountain at an easy jog.

* * *

No sight of any animals on the four miles to the cabin. That box of food had been calling him the whole way home, and he wasted no time eating it. When he finished his early lunch, Jack went into the computer room. He also needed to email Jeff, his press secretary, to see if anything new was happening. Then he would check in with his lawyer Jim to see how the press evasion tactic was going.

But first, it was time to talk to Mick. Talking to Mick always made Jack feel better. The computer program had Mick's personality down exactly right. Sometimes it was as if he was talking to Mick, not a program. Weird as it sounded, Jack felt like Mick was really alive when they were speaking.

When the screen came on, he saw Mick was dressed for running. Mick's first comment was, "Hey Jack, nice suit! It would look better with the hood turned around covering your mug."

Weird, thought Jack. How could Mick have pre-planned a response involving his bodysuit? He must have been aware it was in the works. But he laughed and told Mick about the suit and how it interfaced with the watch and glasses.

"I can see how great it would be to have the two linked," Mick said on the screen. "I wish I had one just like it for my next run."

Startled by what Mick had said, Jack sat back and stared at the monitor. "Are you telling me you still run?"

Mick's image froze and flickered briefly before he answered. "Jack, you can guess I meant figuratively, not really running. I wore different outfits over the years while recording these for you. This time I happened to be in my running gear, so perhaps the AI software added a joke for your entertainment," Mick said with a less than convincing hesitation in his voice.

Still puzzling over Mick's comments, Jack said, "Yah, too bad the AI software can't add the suit to your program. Maybe I should ask Bear if that's possible."

Then Jack changed the subject and talked about the sabertoothed tiger. Mick's image on the monitor looked stressed.

"Jack, in all my years, there has never been anything like this around the crater. If I had known there was such a danger, you would never have run here as a child."

When Jack signed off, Mick's parting words were: "Remember, stay safe and act with wisdom," before the monitor went blank.

As Jack sat in front of the blank screen, questions about Mick's computer program filled his mind. *How on earth could a computer program be so self-aware?*

Later, he said to himself, putting it out of his mind. He still had to contact Jeff and Jim to catch up on the outside world.

A few minutes after sending the texts, Jim wrote back, giving his itinerary and the events in various locations where the press was being dragged. The next stop was Japan because he had always wanted to go there. Jim signed off with, "Thanks for the great vacation, Lobo, see you someday."

Jack couldn't help but smile at Jim's last line. Funny coming from a lawyer who had rarely taken vacations before this.

Jeff, his press secretary, sent a quick note minutes later, mentioning the press following Jim was beginning to get tired. Jeff reminded him that the plan was still in place to get the sabertoothed tiger to move closer to Jack with each encounter while the suit slowly blocked more of Jack's pheromones.

After he read the text, Jack thought about what Jeff had said. If the plan did deceive the big cat, he would be safe. If not, my suit had better be tough.

21

Every morning for two weeks, the big cat followed when Jack ran the trails around the cabin. It always stayed out of sight and downwind, seemingly attempting to become immune to Jack. He knew the cat was there, but nothing caused him alarm. He was beginning to relax, thinking the plan to capture the big cat was working.

One day his college course work completed for the day, Jack went for a run to the crater after his lunch had settled. The sun was hot, and he was looking forward to a swim at the end of the run.

About halfway to the crater, he got a warning on his heads-up display that the big cat was running behind him. The cat was following but not closing in, too far away to be affected by his scent.

Jack kept running, but as he started into the crater, he noticed the big cat had stopped. While he felt relieved, Jack was curious as to why it had stopped.

Then before he had run more than a dozen steps, his glasses started flashing warnings about another large animal up near the top of the crater. Jack looked up to the rim as the readout on his glasses listed the large animal as another sabertoothed tiger. The heads-up display showed the first big cat was still down the trail. This was a second big cat high up on the rim.

Jack tapped a button on his watch for assistance. *Why isn't the lab answering?* Finally, he heard a response.

"We have a visual," one of the lab crew said. "Just freeze. We are analyzing the situation."

Not a problem, Jack thought. *I'm not going anywhere.*

As he waited, Jack thought he'd check out the new big cat using the glasses on the infinity telephoto setting. But when he got sight of the cat, he was honestly sorry he looked.

This cat at the top of the crater rim was bigger than the cat down the trail. It looked older and had more battle scars than the first one. The first cat looked old and tired. This cat looked old but angry. The look on its face was an intense look of pure hatred as it scanned the crater.

Jack was sure the cat had seen him, but it seemed to be looking for something else.

Just then, the lab answered, and Jack jumped.

A technician said, "Jack, we want you to run the lake trail so we can continue to monitor the new cat's actions. Being on the bottom trail will keep you close to the lake for added safety. The suit will protect you from the big cats, but you'll be safer by the water."

"Sounds good to me," said Jack, and he took off running. He ran two laps around the lake and stopped by the bridge as usual for a swim. While taking his shoes off to swim, the lab cut in to say the new cat did not move during his run. Neither had the one down the trail. Their theory was the cats were looking for something other than Jack.

"Keep the suit on, and you'll be safe," said the tech.

Jack enjoyed a refreshing swim and lay in the warm sun, resting on the grass for a while after he hauled out.

As he lay there, the lab checked back in with him, telling him both cats had disappeared. Then the tech asked him an odd question.

"Have you noticed anything different about yourself lately, Jack?"

"Like what?"

"Have you seen any changes in your body? Do you feel bigger?"

"What do you mean bigger?"

"Well, we are getting numbers that show you have grown two inches taller and gained twenty pounds in the last two weeks. We've checked the numbers and they seem to be correct but we are running further tests to see if the suit is sending false information."

"Wow, I haven't noticed. I've only been wearing the suit and haven't worn my regular clothes. But now that I think about it, my shoes do feel a bit tight, and Michelle has just commented that I seemed taller."

"It's too early to know for sure if the suit is out of calibration," said the lab tech. "We will keep running tests and get back to you on it."

As he ran back to the cabin, Jack was puzzled about his recent growth. *Am I really growing? Maybe that's why I've been so hungry lately? Or is it all this fresh air and mountain living? Two inches of growth in two weeks is weird*, he thought. He had to admit he did feel taller and stronger.

The next morning Jack received verifying info from the lab that he had indeed gained twenty-two pounds and a bit over two inches in height. With that news on his mind, he headed down the road to town to talk to Bear and see if Michelle would fix him a big breakfast. After all, he was a growing boy . . .

* * *

Jack snuck in the back door of the café, and Michelle gave him a big smile and a hug when he walked in. She sent him out front with the promise of a meal fit for a hungry wolf. Bear was at a table eating when Jack came out of the kitchen, so he headed there, greeting the regulars on the way.

Bear looked up at Jack and said, "So, it looks as though you are doing a bit of unusual growing, Lobo." Just then, Michelle walked up behind Jack with an armload of food and overheard Bear.

"Yah, remember, I thought you seemed taller," she said as she piled the plates in front of Jack. "Bet it's my healthy cooking," she said, beaming.

Jack looked at Michelle, then at Bear and said, "You might be right about the food."

While he ate, Bear explained the lab had checked all the readings, and it did appear Jack was growing at an accelerated rate that no one could explain. "Your growth doesn't make any sense, even taking Michelle's cooking into account. The doctors at the lab pointed out it is possible to grow at this rate, but it is highly unusual at your age."

"Well, it's alright with me. Before, I was only five foot ten, and I always wanted to be taller."

"The lab will continue to monitor you closely and notify us if anything more happens," said Bear.

* * *

Over the next two weeks, when he was running, the sabertoothed tiger followed him—each time getting closer. He had worn the suit for four weeks, and it was now blocking 90 percent of his pheromones. The big cat should not be gaining immunity no matter how close it got.

Every time Jack ran in the crater, the second cat was high on the rim.

Jack realized he had not heard his guardian since he had seen the big cat up on the crater rim. For reasons unknown by the lab, his high-tech suit was unable to detect his guardian. He could hear it running beside him in the trees, but the suit did not pick it up on any of its scans.

It would be nice to have my guardian running beside me with these big cats around, Jack thought. Not that he did not trust the incredible body suit, but knowing his old running partner was nearby would have been comforting with those two huge cats around. The suit was operating efficiently, it was just a matter of waiting to see what the sabertoothed tiger would do next.

Even though the suit made him feel safe, the feeling of being bait was not comfortable.

The lab told him the cat had stopped trying to get closer, but it was staying near Jack longer. This time while running to the crater, the big cat only ran near him for five minutes, then turned away and disappeared from his scans.

Obviously, it was trying to become immune. The techs believed the cat now thought it had achieved immunity through its movements.

Jack felt a huge relief as he entered the crater and ran across the log bridge for his midday run. He had not run without the second big cat lurking up on the rim for over four weeks, but today the display was not showing the presence of any cats at all.

The first cat had stopped following him a little farther back down the mountain, and the one that was always by the crater rim had not shown on the heads-up display.

What was going on?

He called the lab to have them check his systems for any errors. Within a minute, the lab informed him that the suit and glasses were all operating perfectly. Neither of the big cats was within scanning range.

"Use caution while we continue checking the suit's systems," the tech said.

As he ran toward the middle six-mile trail, he kept his heads-up display scanning. After a mile, he heard a sound that made him happy. It was the sound of his guardian once again following him now that there were no big cats nearby.

"I'm detecting my guardian," Jack told the lab. "See if you can get a fix on it." As usual, the lab could detect nothing of the guardian. After some discussion, they agreed it must be back because the cats were not in the area.

The next task would be to find out why the guardian was avoiding the big cats. Jack let the lab know when the guardian stopped running and where it was at the time. They were trying to figure out where the guardian was coming from now and why it was avoiding the sabertoothed tigers.

Back at the log bridge now, Jack stopped for a cool-down swim before heading back to the cabin. The cool water felt great after the run and helped clear his head.

As he swam, he thought about his guardian. It was nice to have it back, but he was confused about why it hid.

He thought about the many weird things that had been happening. This summer alone, he had found out he was his parents' true son, not adopted, he was a Native American, and leader of his tribe, and filthy rich. There were two sabertoothed tigers following him, and . . . he was talking to his dead uncle and best friend and coach on his computer. Nothing could surprise him anymore.

The run back to the cabin was uneventful and no big cat appeared. As relieved as he was that the cat was not following, Jack was concerned about why it stopped. Why did his guardian always hide when the cats were there? He had many questions about who the guardian was and no solid answers. Why couldn't the latest and best technology ever invented track or even see his guardian?

He thought about talking to Mick, but no way was he ready to talk to him right then. He had too many unanswered questions, and Mick was in many of them.

That evening after dinner, Jack went outside to sit on the porch to enjoy the warmth. He followed orders to always wear the suit unless washing and grabbed the glasses that were on the table by the door as he walked outside. The glasses were fun at night because, using the thermal imaging feature, he could see animals hiding behind bushes. The night was quiet and no animals were around, which he found odd.

After scanning the area again, he saw why there were no animals around. There, over by the river behind the rocks, was the giant sabertoothed tiger. It wasn't moving, and Jack wondered, *Is it sleeping?* It must have thought it couldn't be seen at this distance and behind the rocks.

Why was the big cat that did not come near him today now sleeping nearby? Jack checked in with the lab and they suggested they examine the cat for more information on what it was doing. They would try to extend the range of the suit by adding extra satellites. The hope was to be able to view the big cat from miles away. Maybe they could locate the big cat's den. They would also run the watch recordings from the past few days through the same program to track its past movements.

Jack was not afraid, but he was curious. How could these prehistoric cats be alive anyway? And what did they want with him? What was it about him that made the big cat sick? So many questions and so few answers.

After an hour, the lab suggested Jack head back inside; they would get back to him in the morning with any findings. He glanced at his watch at the image of the big cat behind the rocks and it still had not moved.

Shaking his head in disbelief, Jack headed back into the cabin. He wanted to talk to Mick, but that would probably bring up more questions than answers. Instead, he went in and called Michelle. He knew better than to bring up the big cats and he kept the discussion light so she wouldn't worry. As always, talking to her made him feel better. They laughed, teased each other, and talked about how his studies were going and about food for a while. Before they said good-night, Michelle said, "Be careful running. Come down soon for some home-cooked food instead of whatever you are making for yourself." He promised and wished her a good night.

22

When morning came, Jack felt like he had not dreamed at all. He had promised to stay near the cabin until the lab called. But after last night's restless sleep, running seemed like the best way to clear his head. While stretching outside, he checked for the big cats. Five minutes of scanning while he stretched showed no sign of either cat.

The lab had extended the range of his suit's scanning ability. Used in conjunction with new satellites, they felt confident they would be able to locate the big cat's hideout.

Jack started running down the road to where he first saw the big cat. After a couple of minutes, his heads-up display sounded an alarm. Just then, one of the sabertoothed tigers appeared out of nowhere in the thick trees off to the left.

Before he could speak, one of the lab techs said, "We see him, Jack! We have a visual." The tech told him to stay on the road and avoid the trees until they better understood what the cats were up to. The lab had figured out where the cat came from and was going to investigate further with the satellites and then send in a drone.

Using his heads-up display, Jack watched the big cat approach. It paced him as it ran behind him to the left. The big cat looked incredibly strong as it effortlessly leaped as far as forty feet over logs. As he watched, he thought the tiger was like poetry in motion as it moved. He found the size and strength of the cat intriguing rather than intimidating.

Just then, the sabertoothed tiger turned and suddenly was gone, disappearing as quickly as it had appeared.

Jack's ears filled with excited chatter. The lab techs had just zeroed in on the spot where the cat first appeared and had captured the spot where it disappeared. What sounded like the voices of ten lab techs overtalking each other rang in his ears, and the best he could make out was that the cat had gone into a cave.

A cave would explain how it could appear and disappear quickly. Since the mountain was a volcano, there would be hundreds of caves.

The lab techs' new plan was to map the mountain using satellites to find the caves.

Jack kept running while the lab techs talked. He was approaching the cabin as they were finalizing their plans.

He went for a quick dip in the river to wash, and the techs went back to do their work, so Jack was alone with his thoughts.

If the big cats were using caves and tunnels, they were smarter than anyone could have imagined. "How smart are these things?" Jack said aloud.

"We don't know, but we are trying to figure that out," a tech said, then broke into laughter. "Sorry, Jack," the tech said, still laughing. "When you asked aloud, I assumed you were talking to us."

Jack also got a good laugh, realizing how safe he was with the lab monitoring his moves—and what he said.

In fact, the lab was doing a more thorough job of monitoring him than he knew.

When the communication with Jack cut off, the lab tech asked a supervisor to check the numbers. The lab tech explained how Jack appeared to have grown another two inches and was ten pounds heavier in the last two weeks. Jack had now grown four inches and gained over thirty pounds in four weeks! The supervisor suggested everyone concentrate on finding the answer to how it was possible for him to grow so much.

"Let's keep Jack in the dark until we figure this out," the supervisor said.

* * *

With only one week to go before his college term would start, Jack was getting in as many runs as possible. Today he decided to run to the crater.

After a mile, his heads-up display flashed that the big cat was once again following him. It had now followed him for eight weeks with the cat. His suit has been blocking 90 percent of his pheromones to the cat for the last four weeks as the big cat kept moving closer and closer.

A couple times, when the cat got too close or the wind shifted, it would stumble a bit. The cat moved in and backed off, showing Jack it was still trying to become immune to him. The cat was reacting as if it had not realized Jack's suit was masking his scent as it tried to get closer.

Today the big cat had come as close as ten feet. When Jack turned quickly, he caught the cat off guard. He didn't see it because of the thick brush, but he heard the cat stumble and suddenly run away.

The lab techs and scientists were sure the cat was getting close to making its move, and as Jack watched the sabertoothed tiger quickly close in, he began to wonder, *Is today the day we make contact?*

The big cat was moving toward Jack faster than it ever had before, just as a tech said in his ear, "Be careful!"

Just then, the cat attacked, leaping high and fast toward him. Before Jack could react, his suit started transforming on its own. By the time the cat hit him, the suit had turned solid as armor. The transformed suit had made stabilizer rods going from his waist to the ground, so when the big cat hit him, it was like it hit a tree. It hit his now solid suit with a heavy thud, and the suit released 100 percent of Jack's pheromones.

The big cat staggered back from the impact with the ridged suit. The sudden burst of pheromones caused it to drop to the ground and begin breathing hard.

When the cat fell to the ground, the suit began changing. Jack could tell it was still bulletproof, but he could now move.

Jack began backing away to be safe.

As he did, he saw the cat was having a tougher time breathing, so he backed further away to relieve its suffering.

As he moved away, the cat began moving and tried attacking again but again fell back down.

Jack looked into the golden eyes of the ancient sabertoothed tiger. It was looking straight into his eyes as if it was asking something of him.

Jack carefully observed the scarred giant cat and somehow sensed what it was asking. The cat was tired and wanted to end its incredibly long life of suffering. He didn't know why the cat was trying to attack and kill him, but he knew the big animal wanted to die.

Jack's eyes filled with tears. He knew what the cat was asking of him.

The lab was talking rapidly in his ear, trying to give him instructions, but he knew what needed to be done.

He walked closer to the cat lying there, its giant sides heaving with each labored breath.

As he approached, the cat's breathing grew raspier and faster. Jack paused and bent down. The big cat raised its head and looked directly into his eyes, seemingly pleading to be allowed to die.

With no fear for his safety, Jack stepped closer and put his hand on the cat's tawny shoulder. The big cat touched Jack's hand with its nose and then took a final shuddering breath. The sabertoothed tiger's angry face slowly relaxed into a peaceful stare as its amber eyes closed for a final time.

Jack stayed with the cat until Bear and three others arrived to collect it.

He looked at them but just turned, waved, and ran up the mountain to the crater to be alone with his thoughts.

As he ran, he tried to make sense of what had happened, why the cat wanted to kill him, and why it also wished to die.

He knew the cat was incredibly old and had faced many battles, as it was covered in healed scars, but where did it come from? Why was he poison to the ancient beast?

His troubled thoughts gave him no answers.

23

Lost in his thoughts, Jack was running about a mile from the crater when his glasses began flashing a warning. The other big cat was up near the top of the crater where it had been before.

The crater's upper rim trail was dangerous, so Jack had only run up there a dozen times. Unlike the smooth three- and six-mile trails he usually ran on below, this trail was rough and had steep up-and-down sections alongside a vertical drop into the lake at places.

Jack connected with the lab to see if they had any information on the first cat and to ensure they knew about the second. As Jack reached the crater's lake, the lab informed him that the second cat had shown up on the crater rim edge at the same time as the other cat attacked. It had not moved since then.

"I'm going to head up to the crater rim to see if I can figure out what is happening," Jack informed the lab techs. They weren't happy but felt Jack was safe if he had the suit on. With the lab's approval, he headed up the steep connector trail to the upper rim trail.

He was only a couple hundred feet from the rim when the second big cat stood up, ran down the trail, and disappeared. Jack stopped to talk to the lab and scan the area for any signs of the cat. The lab told him the big cat had disappeared about 400 feet from where it had been lying. They suggested he run to the rim trail to see if he could find where the cat was now.

As he ran, Jack felt good, especially since the suit was performing so well. By the time he reached the rim trail and found the spot where the big cat had disappeared, he had the strangest feeling something was watching him. He stood still and scanned the surrounding area for any signs.

"Is there a problem, Jack?" a lab tech asked.

"Uh, I don't think so. But I have a crazy feeling like something or someone is watching me."

"There's nothing alive near you, but we're keeping the scans on full power."

Jack was looking at the spot in the rock wall where the lab said the big cat disappeared. He saw nothing but solid rock, no openings or caves.

Where has the cat gone? He wondered.

"Jack, we want you to walk up to the rock wall and touch it."

"What are you talking about? Ahead of him was a rock wall with no apparent openings, caves, or doors. Not even a hole in the ground.

"Just humor us. Walk to the wall and touch it," said the tech.

Jack reluctantly walked toward the wall and reached out and touched it. To his amazement, his hand went right through the rock face as if it were air. His hand went up to the wrist before quickly pulling it back out.

"What the . . .!" he hollered as he jumped back. Snickers could be heard in Jack's ear from the lab techs. In his ear, he could hear the lab now erupting with laughter.

"We've figured out the wall has a holographic projection. The big cat simply disappeared into an opening behind it."

"You knew and didn't tell me?"

"We weren't sure, so we waited," the tech answered.

When he had settled down, Jack asked, "So, do you want me to check out the opening behind the holograph?

"We're thinking you should wait and explore the caves later with better equipment and planning, Jack."

Jack again had the creepy feeling at the back of his neck that something was watching him, but it didn't feel dangerous to him. He wondered, *Is my guardian up here somewhere?*

"OK, yeah, I want to run the crater trail anyway. Maybe I'll get a glimpse of my guardian up here in the open."

"Follow your instincts, Jack."

Jack walked to the edge of the crater and began scanning with his glasses for whatever had been watching him. He didn't see any sort of animal or anything out of the ordinary. While he was scanning, he remembered what Mick had taught him about using his senses rather than just the electronics.

He closed his eyes and relaxed. He began to clear his mind of his thoughts and open it to the outside world. As he concentrated on listening to every sound around him, slowly, the sounds began to come to him.

A small mouse moved by a nearby rock. Soon he had located more little animals and insects on the rim around him. Jack focused further away, trying to reach the opposite side of the crater rim.

A faint sound reached him that he recognized. It was the sound of his guardian slowly running across the crater. As he listened, he concentrated on pinpointing its location.

By the sounds, his guardian was exactly opposite him on the middle six-mile-long crater trail. He opened his eyes to locate the guardian. As he expected, he could not see anything, even with his super high-tech gear.

I can hear it, why on earth can't my equipment locate the guardian?

He started running carefully along the upper trail. The trail was very rough, not wide enough to be safe, and dangerous because it had so many sheer cliff drop-offs.

He slowed down, so he was almost walking as he carefully made his way around the crater rim. Only 200 feet around it, alarms went off in his glasses, warning him the second sabertoothed tiger had come out of the cave again. It was running in the opposite direction around the crater rim from Jack, really moving fast and not paying attention to Jack at all.

At first, he did not have any idea where the big cat was going, but then it dawned on him—the cat was running toward his guardian!

It's after the guardian! But why?

He connected with the lab and asked, "Hey, do you have any idea what the big cat is doing?" Worried, he asked, "Do you have a fix on my guardian?"

"We're following the big cat, but we don't have any readings on the guardian."

"Well, somehow, the sabertoothed tiger has a fix on my guardian, even if your equipment can't detect it, Jack said." He told the lab, "I'm headed toward it."

"Affirmative. See if you can head it off."

Jack tried running faster and could feel the suit changing as if it were preparing to protect him from the sharp rocks he was running by. The suit had automatically already added extra padding to the bottom of his shoes for rock protection and ankle bracing against sprains.

Ahead of him, the big cat was moving three times his speed. It was acting as if it had a plan, and Jack was beginning to think it wasn't a good one.

I think it wants to hurt my guardian, Jack thought, his heart beginning to beat faster. Jack relayed his thoughts to the lab and increased his pace.

* * *

The upper rim trail was almost twelve miles around. The guardian was still opposite Jack, meaning a six-mile run over incredibly rough, steep terrain. While trying to increase his speed, Jack ran calculations with the glasses to determine the time it would take him to reach the guardian versus when the sabertoothed tiger would. The calculations showed that at his current pace, the big cat would reach the guardian long before he did.

My guardian's life is at risk. I have to do something to help!

He knew he had to run faster. But he was running on a trail barely wide enough to fit the width of his shoes, and it had rocks the size of oranges covering it.

Time was running out.

Panic was setting in when he thought of a crazy idea.

Jack knew he could control the shape and hardness of the suit, so why not try?

This may be the dumbest thing I have ever done, but I have to try.

Jack relaxed his mind and focused all his concentration on changing the shape of the suit. Then trusting that the suit would perform, he dove off the crater rim toward the lake hundreds of feet below.

Down, down, down he went. Just as he was starting to fall like a rock, the wings took shape. Jack's suit suddenly became alive as it grew wings like a hang glider. He slowed and began moving forward. Instead of falling to the bottom, Jack began gliding toward the opposite side of the crater.

As he was gliding, his glasses told him the guardian on the middle trail was running faster as if it knew the big cat was above it on the upper rim trail closing in fast.

Jack was gliding easily when the guardian took a sharp turn and ran down to the lower lake trail. The big cat was now running down toward the middle trail.

Without warning, Jack's suit started moving on its own. No matter how he tried, he could not control it. He was a helpless prisoner, going for a wild ride as the suit dove toward the lake below.

Then . . . wham! . . . he hit the water at high speed and lost consciousness.

The lab had been monitoring everything since he appeared to dive off the cliff and was now tracking him, passed out in the water, hundreds of feet from the lake shore.

"Jack! Jack! Come in, Jack!" yelled a tech. In the background, one of the others frantically said, "Check his life systems, stat!"

Then the suit began moving on its own toward the shore with Jack unconscious inside, his head kept out of the water.

A lab tech monitoring Jack's bio changes said in a tense voice,

"His temperature is up to 106 degrees. Heart rate is over 220 beats per minute."

And then the bio read-out started to report impossible numbers. Jack was now growing at an incredible rate. In the five minutes since hitting the water, he had grown four inches taller and twenty pounds heavier, and this incredible growth wasn't stopping. By the time the suit had brought Jack to the edge of the lake, he had grown six inches and gained thirty pounds.

Back at the lab, the lab director was frantic. "Check the figures again. What's going on with this rapid growth?" They calculated that he had grown a total of ten inches and gained sixty pounds in eight weeks.

The suit was somehow infusing Jack with everything he needed to facilitate his rapid growth. "We need to investigate fully how the suit is able to do this right now," said the lab director. As far as anyone knew, this was way beyond the suit's original designs. The suit was a self-aware artificial intelligent computer with unknown limitations. Since it was first turned on, the suit has overseen its own programming. Now it was smarter and more powerful than any computer in existence. No one knew the suit's capabilities, but now they were getting an idea of what it could do.

After reaching the shore, the suit walked Jack's body to the running trail as he began slowly regaining consciousness.

Where am I? he thought. *What just happened?* As Jack's mind cleared, he remembered the big cat was heading toward his guardian.

I have to find my guardian. I have to protect it.

Concentrating with all his senses, he found it again. The guardian was now running toward Jack on the lower lake trail only about a mile away.

But then he saw the big cat was chasing it from behind and was about a mile behind the guardian.

I have to get to my guardian, Jack thought and started running. He knew he was slower than the big cat, but he had to try. It did not take more than five or six steps before he realized something was different.

Quick glances at his bio readouts in his heads-up told him something had changed in his body.

If he could believe his readouts, he was taller and heavier than before he jumped off the cliff minutes earlier. He could tell by the speed he was running that he was also faster. Jack tried to make sense of what had happened to him as he ran full speed toward his guardian, but he had no explanation.

The heads-up display showed the sabertoothed tiger was still closing in on his guardian from behind. He calculated that the big cat would reach his guardian seconds sooner than him if he kept running at his current speed. With all his strength and focus, Jack concentrated on running faster. He could feel himself increasing in speed and realized the suit was assisting him.

As he pushed forward and visualized the suit helping him run faster, his speed increased. A glance at the heads-up display showed he was running faster than a world-record sprinter—faster than he had ever run before.

With half a mile still to run, the display showed he was going to reach his guardian just seconds before the big cat would.

He needed a plan.

He called for the lab, and a tech answered immediately, asking, "How are you feeling?"

Jack said, "OK, but what's going on with my bio-readouts?"

The lab explained what they saw on their end and asked, "Do you feel like you have grown, or is it a suit error?"

Still running flat out, Jack said, "I feel bigger, and I know I'm much faster."

As they quickly discussed a plan, the lab advised Jack to run past the guardian and intersect the second sabertoothed tiger. "Release 100 percent of your pheromones now, Jack," the tech advised.

By this time, Jack was sixty seconds from meeting the guardian and big cat. His heads-up display showed his suit was now unsealed. As he closed the last few hundred feet to the guardian, he saw something large running toward him.

But to his shock—it was not the big cat.

24

If it was not the sabertoothed tiger, what could it be?

As he got closer, Jack could finally see the large figure running toward him more clearly. *No way I'm seeing what I'm seeing.*

The large figure speeding incredibly fast toward him looked like an upright hairy ape.

"Are you seeing what I'm seeing?" Jack said to the lab.

A tech gasped, "What is that?"

Before he could answer, Jack saw the sabertoothed tiger come into view 300 feet behind the animal. Jack was now about fifty feet from the large hairy animal that was running toward him.

One of the lab techs yelled, "Bigfoot! It looks like a bigfoot!"

Jack ran right by the large hairy primate, focused on the big cat seconds behind it. He skidded to a stop and steadied himself for the worst just as the big cat leaped toward him.

His suit reacted on its own, suddenly jumping into the air and grabbing the big cat. The tiger and Jack fell to the ground in a tangle of arms, legs, fur, and teeth.

The suit had gotten hard as a rock and had pinned the sabertoothed tiger down so it could not move.

Jack could hear a lab tech in his ear, trying to give instructions, but the suit was in complete control. He couldn't do a thing. It was obvious that the suit was protecting him. Immediately the big cat started breathing heavily and making gasping sounds.

With the big cat immobilized, the suit started releasing its iron grip on the cat. Jack stood up, dusted himself off, and backed away from the suffering tiger.

He could see this sabertoothed tiger was bigger than the other cat and had more scars covering its body. It seemed more aggressive than the other tiger and weak as it was, it kept trying to crawl past Jack to the hairy ape-like thing behind him.

The large hairy animal had run past and stopped a couple of hundred feet away from the big cat. When Jack used the zoom feature on his glasses to focus on the hairy thing down the trail, he was speechless. It looked to him like illustrations he had seen of a type of bigfoot, also known as a Sasquatch, reported to exist in the north-western part of the US.

The bigfoot was just standing there watching Jack.

What do I do now? He looked back and forth between the bigfoot and the hard-breathing tiger. The big cat had almost stopped breathing but still kept trying to get up. It was obvious that the big cat wanted to hurt the bigfoot.

He looked back at the face of the bigfoot when the cat tried again to rise, and he saw fear and anger.

Jack had faced tough decisions before, but this was the hardest, but he knew what he should do. With one last look back at the bigfoot's terrified face, Jack stepped closer to the big cat.

As he came close, the cat looked into his eyes with incredible hatred and breathed its last breath.

Although it had been his enemy, Jack's heart was breaking for the animal. He closed his eyes as hot tears rolled down his cheeks.

When his heads-up display verified the big cat was actually dead, he turned toward the bigfoot and slowly walked its way.

The bigfoot did not move as he approached. When he reached it, Jack could tell by the look on its face that it meant him no harm. Its gentle dark eyes seemed to gleam with intelligence. Jack knew the suit would morph to protect him if needed, but the suit made no modifications.

The Sasquatch looked at him like it wanted to ask a question.

Just then, Jack was startled by movement out of the corner of his eye. Out of the rock face next to the trail came six more bigfoots. As they slowly walked toward Jack, he sensed no threat.

Four of the bigfoots walked past Jack without a word to the body of the sabertoothed tiger. They stood silently over it for a minute, then picked it up and carried it back into the opening of the hidden cave in the rock face.

When they were gone, Jack turned back to the three remaining bigfoots. For what seemed like an eternity, they all stood and stared at one another.

Jack could hear the lab trying to reach him when their signal suddenly went dead.

Not knowing what was going to happen next, Jack realized he wasn't feeling afraid. But what happened next totally surprised him.

A bigfoot stepped close to Jack and gently placed its huge hairy hand on his shoulder, looked at him, then started talking to him in a calm, even tone.

The crazy thing was Jack could understand him. Shocked, he realized the bigfoot was speaking English!

"I am so sorry that you had to kill the sabertoothed tiger," said the large creature as Jack just stared, hardly believing his ears.

The other two bigfoots stood silently as the first one told Jack how the bigfoots had originally genetically engineered the big ancient cats to protect them.

"The cats had always done so until something went wrong, and they started attacking and killing my people for food. We as a species do not kill living beings, so we have spent thousands of years avoiding them and hiding from them."

The Sasquatch told Jack that when his ancestors first arrived 20,000 years before, they discovered humans were poisonous to the big cats.

The first human shaman was much more toxic to the big cats than a normal human.

An ancient bigfoot had asked the shaman if he would patrol the crater so they might again safely venture out and he agreed. For almost 20,000 years, the shaman kept patrol there. About 2,000 years ago, it became apparent the big cats were up to something. After this, only one of the bigfoots was allowed out, and only when a shaman was around.

As Jack stood silently trying to wrap his head around what he was hearing, one of the two bigfoots who had been standing silent stepped closer to Jack.

This one was obviously female, and she also spoke English. Her voice was unexpectedly mild and gentle as she told Jack more of their history with humans.

When she had finished, a third bigfoot stepped forward. This one was also a female; when she talked, it was like soft singing. She said their society had been watching and protecting humans since they first met thousands of years before his tribe first showed up.

"It is now time to present ourselves to the humans outside this mountain," she said. "Jack, we would like you to be our ambassador to the humans once you have learned what is needed."

As Jack stood speechless, she smiled at him and asked, "Would you like a wonderful surprise?"

Still unable to speak, he nodded. When he saw movement to his left, Jack turned and could hardly believe what he was seeing.

He cried out and ran with his arms open as he recognized the people coming out of the same rock face the bigfoot had come from.

Walking toward him were his Uncle Mick, his father, his mother, and his little sister. Shouting and laughing, he took them in his arms, and they hugged him. Tears flowed as Jack embraced each one in turn while the bigfoots stood by in silence.

Mick broke the emotional reunion first. "Please forgive us for the cruel deception, Jack. We could not take the chance that they would go after you to get to us, so we had to make it appear we had been killed. Our fear was that they would do anything to get to me," Mick said.

"I forgive you," said Jack. "I'm just so glad to see you!" The reunion continued with laughing and tears, talking and hugging.

As more of the bigfoot came out to join them, Jack turned to Mick, then gestured to the bigfoot the tiger had been chasing and asked, "Is that my guardian?"

Mick started laughing aloud like only he could. He put a hand on Jack's shoulder and said, "Unbelievably, you are *his* guardian. And from your sudden incredible growth, I believe you might be a surprisingly good guardian too."

Jack took a moment to absorb that. All this time, he had been looking for his guardian to find out *he* was the one who was the guardian.

Now his rapid growth was on his mind. He asked, "What's the deal with my sudden growth anyway?"

But it wasn't Mick who answered, it was the bigfoot Jack once thought was his guardian. Speaking for the first time in a deep, steady voice, he said, "Jack, please accept my most sincere thank you for the years you have spent here. Although you didn't know it, you helped us survive with those cats stalking us."

"As for your incredible growth, well, that was unforeseen. The suit was designed to be self-aware, but we did not expect it to be quite so intelligent. Since it is self-programmed, we did not have any idea what its limitations or capabilities were and still do not after we've seen what it is able to do.

"The suit determined you needed greater size and strength. While you wore the suit, it changed your DNA so it could increase your size. While you were unconscious in the water, it infused your body, gathered needed material from the water and surroundings, and grew you like a plant in a hothouse. Jack, you are now six-feet-eight-inches tall, not much shorter than we are."

"Have I stopped growing, or is there more to come?" asked Jack with a worried look.

The bigfoot smiled and said, "Honestly, we do not know. The suit has a mind of its own."

Just at that moment, Jack's suit formed a small arm with a hand off Jack's left shoulder. As everyone watched, the hand patted Jack's head like a parent patting a kid's head.

"Well, said Mick, "it looks like the suit likes you."

The bigfoot said, "The scans we have run on you show you are in perfect health, just bigger."

Jack's mother, who had been standing next to him, hugged him again and said, "No matter how tall you are, you are still my little boy."

He looked down at his now tiny-appearing mother, scooped her up like a little doll and hugged her tightly before setting her down.

"Well, my little boy," she said, "looks like you have a future as an ambassador to a unique group—once you finish college, that is."

Jack looked at Mick and asked, "Will I still be able to run in college?"

Mick started laughing again and said, "You're so big, I don't think anyone could stop you."

The bigfoot broke in and said, "Your running goals and completion of college are important. Our time is not yet. It will be a dozen more years before we are ready to reveal ourselves to the world of humans."

The female bigfoot who had told Jack the history and his future stepped up to him and said, "I can see in your face and feel what is in your heart. You are worried about your chosen one, whether she will accept you as you are now, and if you have a future together. Worry not, Lobo. Her heart and mind are pure. She shares your love, is completely devoted to you, and desires a future with you. Once you have finished your immediate goals, you two shall be joined and enjoy centuries and offspring together. Michelle will be your partner. Together you two will guide humanity into a partnership with our peoples."

I can't wait to talk to Michelle and tell her all this, and what's on my heart, Jack thought.

The bigfoot then spoke again, "It is time for us to return home, Lobo. Continue your education. When you have finished, we will meet again. You must learn about your history and about our kind. You shall lead humans toward their future and a new world filled with hope, fantastic wonders, and unity. Return to the human world and begin your journey."

Then as he turned to leave, the bigfoot said, "I know you are hurting inside about the death of the two sabertoothed tigers, but be assured, they are not dead. We have them and will repair their damaged DNA. They will live in a protected area where they cannot be hurt or hurt another being."

With that, the little group of bigfoots silently turned, walked into the rock face, and disappeared.

With a sad face, Mick looked at Jack and said, "I and your mother, father, and sister must stay hidden here until everything is safe. Don't worry about us. We are well provided for, with everything we need."

Jack's eyes filled with tears thinking of the coming separation from his family he would have to endure once again.

Mick's own eyes misted as he said, "Jack, you now must return to the real world. You have responsibilities to your goals and our people. You are the chief of our people and will lead the way to our future. Until you have finished college, your duties will be minimal. Jim and Jeff have been keeping things running smoothly and will until you are ready to take over after college.

"They have prepared a schedule for you, including an important press conference ahead. From the look on your face, Lobo, it appears with all the excitement over the last eight weeks, you have forgotten you are now the head of an exceptionally large and powerful company.

Jack looked at Mick and shook his head. "Mick, is there any way I can avoid this?"

"Not a chance," he replied. "Jeff and Jim have made preparations. The college has been informed about the coming year, so everything is ready. The summer coursework you have been doing can now be completed. Our bigfoot friends and the sabertoothed tiger will be the subject of it, minus the advanced science of the Sasquatch. Human society is not ready for a surprise that big," Mick said, chuckling.

"In a dozen years, when you are fully trained, we will begin the process of releasing the truth to humans about our future with the bigfoots."

After more hugs and many tears, they parted. Mick, with Jack's mother and father, and sister, disappeared into the rock face after the bigfoots.

Jack stared at the seemingly impenetrable rock face, then turned and began slowly running back to the cabin and Michelle . . . and his future and the future of his people.

ABOUT THE AUTHOR

Patrick Talmadge Sr. has always been a late bloomer. His growth didn't cease until he was over 21 years old. He reached his pinnacle as a national and world-class masters middle-distance runner at the age of 37, when he won his first master's national track and field championship in the 800-meter run.

At 47, Patrick earned his Bachelor of Arts degree and made history as the oldest NCAA cross-country runner. Seven years later, at 54, he returned to college to pursue a Master's degree in Psychology. During this time, he ran the mile in track, once again setting a record as the oldest NCAA track and field runner. He received his Master's degree in Psychology at 57. At the age of 66, he embarked on his writing journey.

Patrick taught himself to read at the tender age of three and a half and has been an avid reader ever since. With a keen interest in all fields of science, science fiction, and fantasy, he amassed a wealth of knowledge that would later prove invaluable when he began writing. Throughout his 20s and 30s, Patrick devoured two to three books a day. Upon graduating from graduate school in 2011, he retired from competitive running and felt a growing desire to write the stories that had been simmering within him.

In November 2021, spurred on by the love of his life, Patrick began his writing career. By July 2023, he had completed an adult four-book science fiction series about Sasquatch, a four-book children's series on the same subject, and a standalone novel about a senior community that befriends a troupe of Sasquatch.

Patrick possesses a unique ability to write multiple stories simultaneously, allowing him to modify and adjust interconnected narratives for clarity when writing a series. With a bit of luck, Patrick will continue to pursue his passion for writing for the rest of his life, or at least until his computer gives out.

ALSO BY PATRICK TALMADGE

Hidden Mountain Chronicles

Sasquatch Race

Sasquatch Prison Diary

Tenino Caverns

Sasquatch Home Planet

Sasquatch Chronicles

Hunter and Noah vs. Sasquatch Vol. 1

Hunter and Noah vs. Sasquatch Vol. 2

Hunter and Noah vs. Sasquatch Vol. 3

Hunter and Noah vs. Sasquatch Vol. 4

Sasquatch Senior Community Series

Sasquatch Senior Community

Sasquatch Senior Community: Lois and Mel the Beginning

Sasquatch Senior Community: The Early Years

Sasquatch Senior Community: The Middle Years

AFTERWORD

Go to hangaripublishing.com to learn more about the Authors and stay up to date with their newest releases.

www.ingramcontent.com/pod-product-compliance
Lightning Source LLC
Chambersburg PA
CBHW071153120626
46546CB00006B/2244